This is my Book

Robert Karstunen

RAY HURLED HIS BODY FORWARD IN A LONG HOOK SLIDE.

"Home Run Hennessey" (See page 65)

HOME RUN HENNESSEY

or

"Winning the All-Star Game"

by

CHARLES LAWTON

ILLUSTRATED

NEW YORK
CUPPLES & LEON COMPANY
PUBLISHERS

COPYRIGHT, 1941, BY

CUPPLES AND LEON COMPANY

————

HOME RUN HENNESSEY

CONTENTS

iv   CONTENTS

HOME RUN HENNESSEY

CHAPTER I

A NEW OUTFIELDER

THE sharp, staccato sound of wood meeting horse-hide broke the afternoon stillness, and the packed stands reverberated in frenzied shouting. A gleaming white baseball soared out over the diamond. The batter raced down to first base and started for second.

Clarkville School's left fielder pivoted swiftly and sprinted toward the fence. Eager young voices were shouting and yelling, but the fielder paid no heed to the noise. For a moment it appeared that the ball was going to clear the barrier. Then with a frantic leap into the air the fielder flung up his hand.

The ball smacked into his glove and stayed there. But the next moment a groan issued from the stands when the fielder, unable to stop his wild rush, crashed into the fence. The force of the impact spun him around. He swayed dizzily, took a few staggering steps forward, and pitched to the ground on his face.

A substitute player on the Clarkville School bench leaped to his feet. "It's Jim Wells. He's hurt!"

1

"Holy smoke!" exclaimed another lad. "Did you see him crash into that fence?"

Without a word both boys raced across the diamond. They were followed by others. The remaining two Clarkville outfielders had already reached the scene. Then, some of the infielders as well as Clarkville's famous battery, Tom Raynor and Bert West, came up.

"He's unconscious," informed Ros Hackney, tall centerfielder of the Light and Dark Blue nine. "Stand back, fellows. Give him air."

Jimmy Ames, the genial, gray-haired coach pushed through the milling throng. Behind him was stocky Doc Halsey, the school medical attendant and director of the Infirmary. The players spread apart to give the doctor room to examine the injured outfielder.

"What a catch that was!" breathed ruddy-cheeked, good-natured Bert West, the Clarkville backstop.

"It was a honey," agreed Tom Raynor, his lanky battery mate. "He took an awful chance making the catch."

"Hope he isn't hurt badly."

The coach lifted anxious eyes from the prostrate player. A hush had fallen over the stands. Boys from Clarkville and also rooters from Norwood, the opposing team, were straining to see through the knot of players surrounding Jim Wells.

"That was typical of Jim," said the coach seriously. "In fact, it's typical of all you fellows. He always his head and his eyes held a dismal look. His face took on a brighter hue when red-headed Bob Banks, the third baseman, beat out a scratch hit to deep short.

"Wait him out, Ros," directed the coach as the Clarkville centerfielder prepared to move to the plate.

And wait him out he did! After sliding over a sharp-breaking curve for a called strike, Evans had difficulty locating the plate. Two slow balls missed the outside corner and he followed those with two low ones. As a result Ros walked.

Once again the Clarkville rooters took new hope. They began to clamor for a hit. And Ray Hennessey, a left-hander, was up. Ray looked toward Ames, expecting some special order. But when the coach did not even glance at him, Ray realized he was just up there to swing and swing hard.

Many of the Light and Dark Blue students did not know who this new player was. They could not call him by name, but that did not prevent them from urging him to bring in some runs.

"Come on! Paste that apple into the next county!" yelled one leather-lunged baseball addict.

As for Ray, he was very nervous when he toed the rubber and set himself for the first pitch. This was his first game in active competition and he was eager to make good, yet somehow fearful that he might fail. A strange tension gripped him and he felt all his muscles go tight. Sweat began to ooze from his forehead. His hands which gripped the bat handle were clammy. His shoulders jerked a little and he couldn't stop a terrible trembling in his legs.

Evans took a short, abbreviated wind-up and let loose with a fast curve. Ray was over-anxious and misjudged it. He swung savagely and the ball slid past the end of his bat for a strike.

"Take it easy, boy," he cautioned himself. Hollows became quite distinct in his cheeks, and the pressure in his shoulder blades increased.

Evans tricked him with a change of pace and it became strike two. Ray groaned and gritted his teeth. He saw Bob Banks take a long lead off second. Ros took a similar lead away from first. Both boys were ready to run at the crack of the bat. Grimly Ray wondered what the Norwood pitcher's next offering would be.

"All right, Frank!" called the catcher squatting behind the plate. "This chap is duck soup. Feed him the dipsy-doodle!"

Again there was that abbreviated wind-up, the flash of an arm, then the swift passage of a white sphere through space. Every nerve tense, Ray set himself. The catcher had said something about a dipsy-doodle —a slow floater. But something warned Ray this pitch would not be a slow one. And he was right.

The ball hummed toward him, letter-high. Ray swung crisply, waiting till the last instant to snap his wrists. Once again there was the sharp cracking sound of bat meeting ball. Then, Bob and Ros were sprinting around the base paths, heads down, legs beating in an inexorable rhythm.

Ray was rounding first base and legging it for second when he saw the Norwood centerfielder turn his back on home plate and gallop toward the distant fence. The ball was still rising when it cleared the second baseman's head by a margin of five feet and it kept rising.

A furious din of sound floated down across the field from the Clarkville rooting section. It rose to a roar when the ball sailed over the fence for a home run. Every player along the Light and Dark Blue bench rose to his feet to shout and clap as Ray, his face one broad grin of pleasure, rounded third and sped across home plate.

Bob and Ros were waiting for him with outstretched hands.

"Good boy, Ray," stated Bob, giving Ray's hand a vigorous shake.

"That's starting things off with a bang," Ros told him.

Even the coach loosened up enough to say: "Nice hitting, Ray. We needed that."

Ray could only nod and grin again. His face was flushed with joy and exertion. After the cold fear of failure which had seemed to chill the blood in his veins, there had come a warm feeling of comradeship. He was instilled with a new confidence. Somehow, by this one hit, he felt that he really belonged among this fine group of fellows.

Clarkville was in a frenzy of joy now that the home nine had gone into the lead by a score of 3–2. Even when Jack Lowell, who followed Ray in the line-up, flied out to the Norwood right fielder, their spirit could not be dulled. Clarkville was ahead and this promised to be a real ball game.

However, Norwood was not out of the contest. Hank Renson, the visiting catcher proved this when he led off with a screaming triple between Ray and Ros in left centerfield. Only a brilliant one-handed pick-up of the bounding ball out near the running track, and a horneting throw in to Bert West kept Renson from stretching it into a four-bagger.

Tom Raynor worked carefully on the next batter and got him to pop up to Bob Banks at third. But the next player stepped into a fast curve and sent it to deep right centerfield. Jack Lowell made a fine running catch but his throw-in was too late to nip Renson who scored standing up. And so the count was deadlocked at 3–3.

Tom retired the next batter on a slow roller down to Charlie but the damage had been done. When Clarkville failed to get a man to first in the sixth or seventh, while Norwood continued to threaten in each inning, the loyal Light and Dark Blue rooters began to worry.

It took a leaping one-handed catch by Stumpy Pete
Smith at second to pull Tom out of a hole in the seventh. There were two men on base at the time with
one out. Pete speared the liner and stepped on second
to double the runner who was already halfway down to
third.

But in the eighth Tom failed to get out of trouble
so easily. The first Norwood batter went down via the
strikeout route but Jim Belton, the centerfielder,
dropped a fluke double down the right field foul line.
On the first throw to Ed Frankel, the latter connected
for a solid single into left field.

Ray charged in for the ball and took it on one
bounce. A swift glance revealed to him that Belton was
rounding third and headed for home. Ray straightened and sent the ball humming to Bert West. Bert
was set for it at home plate. Belton was racing down
the baseline, but just as he hit the ground in a hook
slide, Bert snared the ball and slapped it on him.

"Out!" yelled the umpire, jerking his thumb up in
the air in a decisive gesture.

It had been a close play and it kept a run from
scoring. However, on the throw-in Frankel had scampered around to second. Any kind of a hit would
bring him in. Tom put on the pressure and managed
to retire the next batter on a pop-up to Bert. But it
was obvious to everyone that Tom was tiring. He had
recently recovered from an illness and was not yet at
full strength.

He had trouble with his control when he faced Hank Renson. Three times he missed the inside corner with fast curves. Then, forced to put one in the groove, he came through with a high hard one. Instead of letting this "automatic" strike go by, Renson leaned on it and poled it over Jack Lowell's head for a long double that scored Frankel and put Norwood in the lead once more.

George Rassas, who followed Renson, lofted a towering fly to Ray who camped under it for the final out of the inning.

The Clarkville players rushed in from the field and Bert assailed them with his eager chatter.

"Let's get that run back, fellows!"

Charlie Minor came up and spoke to Tom. "How's the arm?"

"Hurts a little. Guess I need more work before I'll be able to go the full nine innings without trouble."

"Just bear down for one more frame and we'll come out on top," said Bert who was always an optimist. He turned to Ray. "Ros is up first. If he gets on base, you bring him in with another homer."

Ray grinned. "I'll be aiming for the fences."

Jimmy Ames overheard the remark. He spoke seriously. "Just hit safely. That's what counts, Ray."

"I know," said Ray, his strongly chiseled face sobering instantly. "I wasn't trying to hit a home run before. I just hit it and it went over the fence."

The talk was cut off when Evans finished his warm-up pitches and Ros stepped into the batter's box. He missed a low, sweeping curve, failed to nibble at another low one which was called a ball, then timed Evans' change of pace beautifully to punch a safety over second base.

"Hit another homer!" sang out the Clarkville rooters as Ray took his firm stance in the batter's box again.

The call was like rich wine in his blood. He flushed with pleasure. His jaw hardened and he made a silent vow that he would hit safely. He wasn't going to aim for the fences. No. He was just going to hit and get on base.

"Think you can do it again, Hennessey?" queried Renson, the Norwood catcher as he gave the signal to Evans.

"Wait and see," responded Ray evenly, not once taking his eyes from Evans.

CHAPTER II

Evans' pitch roared toward the plate, hard and fast. Ray brought his bat around in a swift, savage arc. He felt the impact of the hit and raced toward first. Halfway down the base path he halted as the ball sliced far to the right and went foul.

In the batter's box again, Ray rubbed some sand on his hands and took a firm grip on the willow. The next toss sped across the outside corner of the plate, curving wide. It was the kind of ball Ray liked— waist-high and outside near the end of the bat. His swing was smooth and effortless.

For a moment it appeared the curving sphere would dip past the swishing wood. Then the solid smack of bat against ball rang through the air and a white bullet zoomed toward the outfield. Both the centerfielder and leftfielder dug in their spikes and pounded toward the running track.

The Clarkville fans were yelling shrilly. They stood up on the benches, waving their arms, stamping their feet. Ray scooted down to first and raced for second, slowing up when he saw the outfielders halt their futile dash and watch the ball drop over the fence. A din

14

of shouting was in Ray's ears as he circled the sacks and it was like music to him.

He crossed the plate in a daze. Clarkville players were shaking his hand and he was not aware of it. Evans, the Norwood pitcher, threw his glove on the mound in disgust.

"Brother when you hit 'em, they certainly stay hit!" stated Ros, slapping Ray on the back.

"That puts us back in the lead," said Bert jubilantly, dancing up and down as Jack Lowell prepared to face Evans.

Ray returned to the bench with Ros and Tom and Bert all talking and laughing in jubilation at the sudden change in Clarkville's fortunes.

"That was timely hitting, Ray," said Ames, his face serious as he turned to watch Jack Lowell swing and miss a slow curve.

But if the Light and Dark Blue players thought they were going to have a big rally at the expense of Norwood, Evans soon changed their minds. He tightened up at once and retired Jack, Bert and Bill Prudy, the shortstop in one-two-three order.

Everyone was tense as Norwood prepared to bat for the first half of the ninth. The same question plagued Clarkville players and rooters alike. Could Tom pitch his way safely past this inning despite the very obvious fact that he was tired, and that only great defensive play by his teammates had kept the Norwood score down to what it was?

The first man to hit for the visitors dribbled a roller down to Tom to the right of the pitcher's box. Tom raced over, scooped up the ball and rifled it to Charlie Minor. Charlie leaped high in the air to snare the ball but the runner was safe, having touched the bag while the Clarkville first baseman was leaping to bring down Tom's poor throw.

"All right, Tom, get two this time!" yelled Ray from left field. "Let's salt this game away."

And Tom really gave everything he had to send the next batter back to the bench on three straight strikes. However, the following hitter pickled one of Tom's sweeping slants and sent it humming between third and short. Bob Banks made a frantic dive for the ball as it screamed past his reaching fingers.

Ray came in very fast to pick up the ball and whip it over to Bob who raced back to cover third as the runner from first slid in safely. The Clarkville coach rose from the bench and began to pace up and down. He glanced toward Tom as if he were contemplating removing him from the hill, then signalled for him to resume pitching.

"Talk it up in there, gang!" yelled Ray, every muscle tense and eager for the next play.

He knew that if a ball was hit out to him he would have to be fast because that runner on third would do his best to score. Somehow Clarkville had to cut off that run at the plate.

Ray breathed easier when the Norwood second baseman lifted a pop foul high into the air. Bert threw off
his mask and trundled halfway down the first base line
to take it for the second out.

Still, the inning was not over. There were runners
on first and third with two out and Evans was due to
hit. The Norwood pitcher started toward the plate,
then was called back. There was a flurry of activity
around the visitors' bench. At last, a player in a fresh
uniform strode up to take Evans' place. Norwood was
sending in a pinch hitter to bring home that tying run!

Tom took a lot of time with the batter. He tried to
make him go for two wide ones, but the boy at the
plate could not be fooled. Then, with two balls and
no strikes on him, the pinch batter muffed Tom's screw-
ball. Tom tried the same pitch and missed the outside
corner for another ball. Gritting his teeth, Tom fired
a fast one right down the middle which the batter let
go by.

The runners took generous leads off their bases.
This was a full count and with two out they would be
moving with the pitch. Ray smacked a clenched fist
into his glove and waited. A hush fell over the stands.
There was a short wind-up, the flip of Tom's arm, the
shooting white bullet arcing through the air, then
smashing back over the infield as the batter connected.

Ray left his position deep in left field at the crack
of the bat. His spiked shoes made a steady beat on the

turf as he raced in fast for this low looping liner that threatened to fall in short left for a Texas leaguer. Bob Banks scooted back and far to his left in a frantic attempt to fling his glove on the liner but missed.

Breath was churning from Ray's lungs as he pounded on. He gasped as he saw the ball dropping, dropping. He was close to it, but would he get close enough to put his glove on it? Desperation impelled him to make one supreme burst of effort. Throwing himself forward, arms outflung, head low, he clutched the plummeting ball at his shoe tops.

A roar went up from the stands. Ray didn't hear it. He had the ball in his glove and he gripped it firmly as he struck the ground on his shoulders and somersaulted once to pitch to his knees. But most important of all was the fact that he still clutched the ball. This was the final out and Clarkville had won 5 to 4!

One after the other, spiked shoes clattering on the cement floor, the weary but jubilant Clarkville players trooped into the gym. Outside the warm Spring air rang to the shouts and cries of students coming from Alumni Field.

Ray and Ros and the rest of the "Corbin bunch" as they were called by players who resided in other halls and dormitories on the campus, were stripping off their uniforms and preparing to take showers.

Seated on a bench, Ray let one spiked shoe drop to the cement floor and began peeling off a sock.

"You played like a house afire," said Ros with a warm smile of admiration for his chum.

The tall, sandy-haired lad grinned, his cheeks reddening slightly. "Guess I was just lucky."

"Lucky nothing," protested Bert, stowing his catching paraphernalia in his locker. "You were practically the entire team. Without you Clarkville wouldn't have had a chance."

"Bert's right," agreed Charlie Minor. "The score was 5 to 4 and you drove in all five runs with your two homers. You made several corking catches. And that last one which ended the game was a humdinger!"

"Cut it out, fellows," protested Ray, his eyes twinkling. "You'll be giving me a swelled head."

"You deserve to have one," said Ros. "Why, you're whaling the ball farther than even Bert could do in his prime!"

Chubby Bert West made a lunge for Ros who laughed and skipped toward the showers. "What do you mean in my prime? Wait till I get my hands on you, fellow!" But Bert was grinning as he said it and soon came walking back to join Ray, Tom and Charlie.

Tom saw the slightly puzzled frown on Ray's face and began to enlighten him.

"No kidding, Ray, Bert used to be our home run hitter. Last year he pounded those fences plenty. But this year Coach Ames did some work on Bert and decided he was too timely a hitter to concentrate his efforts on distance. As a result, Bert is getting many more hits than he did last year, even though he doesn't drive them as far. A little change in stance and more accurate timing and placing did that."

"But I'll never be missed as a slugger," said Bert, laughing, "as long as Ray can clout the apple like he did against Norwood."

Those of you who have read the previous volumes in this series written around the stirring activities of a group of adventure-loving boys attending Clarkville School, will recall the thrilling times enjoyed by Tom and Bert in the book entitled, *Clarkville's Battery*.

In that volume Tom and Bert did yeoman work in a damaging flood that inundated the entire state. Trapped in a store with the water lapping at their chins, they were rescued by school chums. Later, they were kidnapped by gangsters interfering in scholastic baseball. The account of their daring escape, their successful attempt to prevent a little boy from being kidnapped by the same gang, and their final crowning achievement of being recognized as Clarkville's star battery offers breath-taking reading thrills.

Following that volume was *Ros Hackney—Halfback*, the story of a courageous football captain who was cast in a role for which he was not fit, yet still managed to make good despite the evil schemes of a disgruntled teammate.

Then, there was *The Winning Forward Pass*, a mile-a-minute gridiron yarn featuring Jack Lowell, a new triple-threat Clarkville ace. The thrills pile up page after page as Jack leads his team to an undefeated, untied season and a chance in Miami's Orange Bowl to fight for the National Scholastic Football Championship.

It was Jack Lowell's sensational passing, his quick-thinking and efficient execution of trick plays that helped the Light and Dark Blue eleven through their season. And during the season there was trouble with players from another school, a mysterious robbery from the library while Jack was supposed to be assistant night watchman. Then, when Clarkville won the right to go to Miami, the Clarkville team was snowbound high in the mountains in a big streamlined bus. They became involved with a gang of international agents intent on stealing valuable United States plans. Jack and his friends took a daring risk but won out in a stirring trek through the blizzard. They brought the foreign agents to justice and then swept on to victory in the Orange Bowl game.

"Seriously, Bert," queried Ray who had lapsed into a strained, troubled silence, "do you think I'll be good enough to stick on the team in Jim's place?"

"Good enough? Why, Jim would have a tough time keeping his position even if he could play."

"But maybe I was lucky."

"Gather around, everybody!"

This was the Clarkville coach calling the players in a huddle for an after-game pep talk. Boys began streaming out of the showers, towels wrapped about their gleaming middles. Others in underwear or still in their uniforms, crowded close to Jimmy Ames.

"Maybe you'll get your answer now, Ray," Tom told him as they joined the eager throng of boys.

The gray-haired baseball mentor waited until the din of noise had ebbed, then addressed his charges in quiet, incisive tones.

"All right, boys, we won a ball game today. But don't let that fool you. It was close, and if it hadn't been for some good fielding we easily could have lost it. You chaps aren't hitting. In case you don't realize it, Norwood was supposed to be the easiest team on our schedule. From now on the games will be tougher."

Ames paused and let his penetrating glance rake the silent, sober group ringed about him.

"I want to see more pepper out there," he resumed. "Show some spirit. That Norwood pitcher wasn't any great shakes. Yet, only Ros Hackney, Ray Hennessey and Bert West managed to get two hits. In fact, our total of base knocks was seven. Norwood outhit us ten to seven.

"Next week I'm calling for intensive batting drills. And don't any of you think because you've been regulars on the team that your position is secure. If you fellows are not up to par, you'll warm the bench. You all know what the schedule calls for. After today we face St. Luke's, Springfield, Bridgeport, Walton, Glendale, Greenwich, and Stamford. Springfield has a crackerjack outfit. They've got excellent pitching, hitting and fielding. Coming so early in the season, that game will likely ruin our season—unless you fellows perk up."

"I reckon part of the blame can be placed on my shoulders," offered Tom, reddening as his teammates turned to listen to him. "I wasn't myself. Didn't seem to have my control."

Ames nodded. "Right you are. However, that may not be entirely your fault. You've been ill. That whip of yours needs more work. I want you to rest it completely for two days, then take daily workouts. I'm not going to use you against St. Luke's. I want to be sure you're in tip-top shape for that Springfield contest when you'll have to face Bart Himber."

"Himber made the New England All-Scholastic team last year didn't he, coach?" queried Bert.

"That's right. He's very good." Ames halted, his gaze swinging to Ray and lingering on the boy. "Ray, you played good ball today for your first time in active competition on the team. I'd like to see you keep it up."

"Will I play against St. Luke's?" asked Ray, his voice taut with strain.

"I can't see why not. Only remember what I said. Don't aim for the fences. Those home runs meant the ball game for us, but there are times when a solid single is just as welcome."

Ray flushed. "Yes sir, but I don't try to hit home runs. I just swing at what looks good."

"Glad to hear you say that," murmured Ames. His bronzed features showed faint pleasure. "I thought as much. You're a natural hitter and you get a lot of power in your drives. Just keep plugging. And that goes for all of you. St. Luke's is next and then Springfield. And if we take Springfield I may be able to promise a surprise—for some of you, at least."

"What is it, Coach?" chorused the squad.

Ames held up his hand. "Not now, fellows. Later —after we lick the Springfield Reds."

"We *will* beat them!" affirmed Bert.

"You bet we will," said Ray and Ros together, both caught up with a strange fervor.

CHAPTER III

INTENSIVE batting drills were held by Coach Jimmy Ames out on Alumni Field each afternoon when classes were over. Ray and Ros, Tom and Bert and all the others never missed a practice. All the regulars were anxious to hold their posts on the team, while Ray was eager to win recognition from Ames as a regular.

Gradually under the watchful eye of the Clarkville mentor the players began to hit better. Their timing improved and they were placing their blows in the spots they aimed at. The right-handed pull hitters were rifling their hits into left field. By the time the St. Luke's contest arrived the Light and Dark Blue nine appeared to be a vastly improved organization. And they were!

Clarkville, going to work on the visiting pitcher in the very first inning, rolled up four runs. Ray climaxed this furious outburst with a three-run homer which followed successive singles by Bob Banks and Ros Hackney.

Coach Ames decided to take a chance on the mound with Jack Lowell who served as outfielder and utility

25

pitcher. Ames had been working all during the weeks of practice with Jack, helping him with his control and his change of pace. And though he lacked the finesse and speed and control of Tom Raynor, Jack turned in a creditable job of pitching.

After weathering a stormy first inning in which St. Luke's drove in three runs, and then loaded the bases before finally being retired, Jack settled down.

The game was a free-hitting affair with Clarkville finally winning 12 to 5. The Light and Dark Blue nine chalked up sixteen safeties while St. Luke's garnered ten which Jack, with the aid of some excellent support, managed to scatter fairly well.

Once again Ray was the batting star of the game, getting two home runs and a double in four official trips to the plate. He drove in five runs and handled seven chances in the outfield without a miscue.

However, the intensive drills continued even after the St. Luke's victory because Ames was really worried about the approaching contest with Springfield. Tom worked out daily, exercising his arm and building himself up. All the others looked better. By the time the day of the big game arrived Doc Halsey pronounced that Tom was ready to pitch the full nine innings. As for the rest of the team, they were a peppy outfit when they took the field for practice.

The Springfield players trooped slowly off the diamond as the Light and Dark Blue squad prepared to take their place.

"Come on, Ros," yelled Ray over his shoulder. "Let's get out there and shag some flies."

Ros answered something unintelligible and then Ray was jarred by the sudden impact of a collision with another boy. He pitched backwards, then regained his balance.

"Sorry," he murmured, grinning pleasantly.

"Why don't you look where you're going?" came the surly question.

Ray stiffened and his eyelids dropped a notch while he surveyed the dark-haired, arrogant boy who faced him. From photos he had seen in local newspapers Ray recognized the boy as Bart Himber, Springfield's sensational pitcher.

Bart Himber was six feet tall, thick in the shoulders and chest. He had smoky, unpleasant gray eyes and thin lips which held a curl of contempt.

"I said I was sorry," repeated Ray, striving to keep anger out of his voice.

Ros passed them with a sharp glance. "Come along, Ray."

Bart Himber snorted derisively. "So you're Ray Hennessey."

"That's right. And you're—"

"I'm Himber—guess you've heard of me," snapped the other lad, his eyes cold and hostile. "Supposed to be quite a home run hitter, aren't you? Well, I'm going to scare the pants off you."

A slow temper began to simmer within Ray but he

kept his voice even and well-controlled. "I wish you luck, friend."

With that Ray turned and walked off, but not before he again felt the full, solid impact of Bart Himber's smoldering gaze. An instant hostility had sprung up between these two boys. It distressed Ray because he was naturally friendly but at the moment he could do nothing about it.

Fifteen minutes later the game got under way. Springfield went to bat first. The Green and White nine managed to get a man as far as second by virtue of a single and an infield out, but Tom turned on the juice and retired the side without any runs.

Dark, heavy clouds were scudding across the sky when Clarkville came in for its half of the first frame. The air was damp with a hint of impending rain in it.

"Looks like it's going to sprinkle," observed Charlie Minor as he strode to the plate.

Bob Banks answered him briefly. "Well, let's sprinkle some base hits around the diamond."

Out on the mound big Bart Himber finished his warm-up pitches with a flourish. His first toss to Charlie was a fast one, high and inside, making the Clarkville lead-off batter duck away. After that Himber proceeded to fan Charlie on three successive pitches.

Charlie approached the bench, a gloomy look on his face. "By gosh, I'm not sure, but I think that Himber chap was 'dusting' me off with that first throw."

"He'd better not try that in this league," muttered Ros.

"Look at that!" exclaimed Ray as Bob Banks spun around and fell to the dirt as he scampered away from a hot one that had come dangerously close to his head. "Himber *is* throwing bean balls."

Ames heard the remark. "Better not judge too hastily, fellows. He may be having trouble with his control."

Ray and Ros did not answer but their faces grew stern. They could hear Fred Dressen, the Springfield backstop, trying to bait Bob with nasty remarks.

The count went to two-and-two and then Bob failed to duck away fast enough from a wide ball and was struck in the ribs. He trotted down to first, and Ros stepped up.

If Himber had been having trouble with his control against Charlie and Bob, he suddenly regained it against Ros. Himber was unusually fast. He had a fine, sharp-breaking curve, a good slow ball and a very deceptive delivery. Ros found that out when he swung too soon on a lazy floater for a third strike.

Ray took his favorite bat and strode to the plate, grinning at Ros who shook his head ruefully at his own failure to get a piece of the ball.

"Come on, Ray!" called Bob, taking a lead off first. "Salt that old apple away."

"Hello, sucker!" said Himber, scuffing the dirt

around the hill with the toe of his spiked shoes while he gave Ray a narrow-lidded, insolent stare.

Ray met the glance evenly and said nothing. He tightened his grip on the willow and dug in, prepared to give the ball a ride if it came in the right spot. The next moment he had fallen to the dirt as a screaming fast one shot like a bullet toward the side of his head.

The ball slapped into Dressen's mitt with a sharp smack and Ray got up, dusting off his uniform pants.

"What's the matter? Scared?" jeered Dressen. The latter was a chunky red-headed lad with cold gray eyes, a pointed nose and thin almost bloodless lips.

"I hope that was an accident," said Ray quietly.

"And if it wasn't?" queried Dressen softly.

"Wait and see."

Again the pitch came horneting toward the plate. And again Ray stepped backward as the ball seemed to rocket dangerously near his head. But at the last moment he saw the ball dip and curve across the inside corner while the umpire signalled that the pitch was a strike.

"So you're Clarkville's home run hitter!" taunted Himber. "Try this one!"

He took his intricate wind-up, cocked his arm back and let loose with a half-speed pitch that caught Ray napping and it was two strikes. Ray topped the next one and sent a hot grounder down to the second baseman which the latter took on one hop, then flipped to the shortstop to force Bob coming into the bag.

The second and third innings rolled by without further incident. Springfield got a runner to second in the third by virtue of a fluke double but the next two men popped up and that threat was killed. In the meantime Clarkville went down in one-two-three order. Except for Bob Banks who had been hit by a pitch, no one had been on base. At intervals Himber would uncork a throw that appeared to be a duster, and then he would settle down to pitch remarkable ball.

In the fourth Springfield broke the scoreless spell. With one out Jim Cresset, the Green and White second sacker sent a low looper over third. The ball skidded along the foul line and Ray made a wild dash to retrieve it. His throw to Pete Smith at second was perfect but Cresset beat the toss easily.

Fred Dressen came up, then, and pasted Tom's first offering over Ros' head in centerfield and by swift running stretched it into a triple. A long sacrifice fly brought in Dressen before Tom succeeded in retiring the side. And so Springfield led 2 to 0.

Himber breezed past Bob Banks, getting him on a foul pop to Dressen, but lost Ros trying to cut the corners too fine and the latter got a base on balls.

"Here's your easy mark, Bart!" called Dressen as Ray came up and toed the rubber.

"I'm going to make you look sick," warned Himber.

Ray's chin lifted and his eyes flashed angrily. "Play ball, Himber. You talk too much."

The Springfield hurler snorted and his shoulders

lifted in a gesture of rage. His first pitch hummed toward the plate with the speed of a bullet. Himber was so angry he meant to burn the ball right past Ray. That was his mistake.

The ball came in like a bullet and shot out over the infield in the same manner. Everyone in the stands rose and a shout rippled through the air as the ball gained altitude. Fielders were running toward the fence, then they halted and watched the gleaming pellet carom off the trunk of a tree on the far side of the fence.

There was a broad grin on Ray's features as he jogged around the bases. He turned toward Himber as he rounded third and his talk slapped at the boy, crisp and vindictive.

"Who's sick now?"

Himber made no answer. He kicked angrily at the dirt and turned to take a new ball which Dressen threw to him.

"Ray, you sure fixed that chap's wagon," breathed Bert as Ray was surrounded by Clarkville players and pounded on the back.

"It took the wind completely out of his sails," said Tom. "Look!"

There was the sharp crack of bat meeting ball and the chums whirled to see Jack Lowell sprinting down to first and then racing to second as he parked a two-base hit in deep center field.

CHAPTER IV

ON THE SPOT

WHEN the speeding baseball thumped against his skull, Ray was conscious of a blinding sense of pain. A red mist swam before his eyes. There was a dull roaring in his ears and an explosion seemed to be set off within his head. After that darkness enveloped him. When he came to he found himself in a clean-sheeted bed in the Infirmary in the same room with Jim Wells.

"Welcome home, Ray," Jim greeted him with a grin. "Misery loves company. This place was getting too lonesome."

Ray's eyes blinked at the unaccustomed light and then he saw the host of friends around his bed. He knew, then, that he hadn't been out long because Tom and Bert and Ros were still in their mud-caked uniforms.

"Thank God, you've come out of it," breathed Tom. "When I saw you fall and lie so still I thought you—you—" Tom didn't finish but each boy in the room knew what he meant.

"How do you feel?" queried Bert tensely.

"There's a buzzing noise in my head. In fact, I feel

as if there's a thousand little gnomes pounding away inside my skull with their hammers."

"That was some whack you got," said Ros.

"Himber deliberately beaned him!" stated Bert.

"It sure looked like it," agreed Tom. "He dusted Charlie and Bob off in the very first inning."

"If I could have gotten my hands on that chap I think I would have torn him apart."

"The coach saw how wild you were and he stopped you," said Ros.

"But what about the game?" demanded Ray weakly. "We didn't lose, did we?"

"No," said Bert. "It wound up in a 4—4 tie. The umpires called it in the tenth when it started to pour. The field got like a quagmire."

"We'll have to play it over, then."

"Not unless both Springfield and Clarkville are undefeated at the end of the season," put in Ros.

A heavy step sounded in the hall and genial Doc Halsey, black bag in hand, entered the room.

"What are you boys doing in here? You'll have to clear out at once!" he roared and for the moment he appeared to be displeased. "Ray needs quiet and rest. He may be seriously hurt. I've been waiting for him to regain consciousness. I'll have to take X-rays to make sure he hasn't suffered any serious injury."

"Sorry, doc," said Bert. "We just wanted to see how he was."

"All right. Get out now. I'll let you know when it's all right to visit him."

With Doc Halsey hurrying them along, Ros, Tom and the others soon disappeared. Fortunately for Ray, the X-rays revealed no skull fracture. There had been a very slight concussion, but after a few days of forced rest and quiet in the Infirmary he was allowed to return to his regular classes. However, it was a full week before the doctor would permit Ray to play baseball. As a result, Ray joined the team in their bus trip to Bridgeport without having had any practice all week.

In the very first inning the Light and Dark Blue nine started to work on the Bridgeport flinger. Charlie Minor led off with a safe bingle, went to second on Bob's infield grounder and to third on a surprise bunt by Ros. And so Ray found himself at bat with two gone and a runner on third. For some reason he felt a trifle strange at the plate. A vague sense of uneasiness pervaded his senses. He could not account for the reason.

He gripped the bat firmly in his hand and faced the pitcher. The ball came in hard and fast. It was an inside pitch, chin high and Ray ducked out of the way though there was no danger of the ball striking him. He swung feebly at the next one and then fouled out to the third baseman as he lunged away from another inside ball.

In the last half of the second Bridgeport broke into the run column when Ace Malone, the slugging right fielder, walloped a fourmaster far over Ros' head. Clarkville came up for the third frame and Bob Banks led off with a single. Ros lined one deep to Malone before Ray came up again.

He faced the Bridgeport flinger and suddenly sweat began to ooze from his forehead. His hands were moist and clammy. There was a distinct pallor on his cheeks. It made his face thinner, turned his eyes feverish.

A white sphere whistled through the air. Ray stepped back then lunged at the ball as it curved outward and away from his bat for a swinging strike. He was trembling and with an alarming certainty Ray knew the answer. He was afraid! Yes, he dreaded each pitch that came toward the plate.

He choked back a sob of futile rage at himself. What had come over him? There was nothing to be afraid of. And yet he stood here in mortal dread of the next pitch. A cold wind seemed to fan up and down his spine, and his throat was parched and dry.

There it was again! That horrible twisting, twirling object. It seemed to make faces at him. It came straight toward him. He felt himself go weak all over. All energy drained from his limbs. Somehow he backed away from the ball.

"Strike!" intoned the umpire.

The next one roared in over the plate waist-high and barely cutting the inside corner. Again Ray stepped back and again the umpire called it a strike. Desperation girded Ray into swinging at the next pitch which proved to be a wide, sweeping curve. The Clarkville rooters who had accompanied the team groaned as Ray trudged dejectedly back to the bench.

On the way to the outfield Ros and Jack moved into step beside Ray. There was a troubled frown on Ros' cheeks.

"What's eating you, Ray? You're swinging like a rusty gate."

Ray was a picture of misery. There was a deep, dismal hurt in his eyes but he could not bring himself to answer his chum.

"If I didn't know you," said Jack slowly, "I'd say you were acting as if you were scared."

"I *am* scared!" blurted Ray.

"Ray, you don't mean that!" Ros stopped in his tracks and his strong fingers gripped both of Ray's arms above the elbows.

"It's true," said Ray, misery dripping from every word. "I dread every pitch that comes toward the plate. I don't know what's come over me. While I'm sitting on the bench, I'm eager to get up and hit. But the moment I'm up there and facing the pitcher and that ball comes toward me, a cold sweat covers me from head to foot."

Jack whistled in amazement. "Say, maybe you're sick."

"I'm disgusted with myself," grunted Ray. If it had

been anyone else save his close friends he would have never admitted his fear. He was ashamed of it, yet it was something he had to talk about.

"We'll talk this over later," directed Ros seriously. "Come on, Tom's ready to go. Get to your positions."

All three boys took up their proper stations in the outfield and the game was resumed. It proved to be a dull, uninteresting contest. Bridgeport tallied another marker in the fifth on a walk, a perfect squeeze bunt and a timely single, and led 2 to 0.

Clarkville was finally roused from its lethargy and got that run back in the first of the sixth. With one down Ros doubled to left field. Ray tried desperately to hit safely but that strange fear still gripped him and he struck out. However, Jack Lowell followed with another double to score Ros.

In the seventh the Light and Dark Blue tied it up on Pete Smith's single and Tom Raynor's triple. Tom then proceeded to set Bridgeport down in the last half of the seventh and in the eighth Clarkville threatened again.

Bob Banks drew a base on balls to start the frame and Ros lined to deep left. Ray started for the plate and was recalled at the last minute by Ames who directed Al Larson to pinch hit for him. And Larson delivered a screaming two-base hit to tally Bob all the way from first and sew up the ball game 3 to 2. And that was the way the score remained.

Tom pitched air-tight ball in the eighth and ninth

with the result that the victorious Clarkville nine raced jubilantly toward the showers.

"Still undefeated, boys!" shouted Bert.

"Let's keep it up all season!" yelled Pete Smith.

Ray was one of the last players to reach the dressing rooms. His broad shoulders slumped and his feet dragged when he walked. Despair was written in every weary line of his rugged face. The black cinders of defeat drenched any spark of energy that might have been in him.

Ros, Tom, Bert, Jack and Charlie all grouped around Ray in an attempt to break his dark mood.

"Cheer up, Ray," urged Charlie. "We all have bad days. No reason to feel so miserable."

"You don't know the half of it," murmured Ray, finding little comfort in this talk.

Bert pushed his ruddy face close to Ray. "That true what Ros tells me about you being scared up at the plate?"

Ray nodded gloomily, a bitter smile planing down from his lips. "It's true. Go ahead. Say what you think. I'm disgusted."

"But what's come over you?" Bert persisted.

"I wish I knew," groaned Ray.

"I'll bet it was just the long lay-off after being beaned," said Tom.

"Wait!" exclaimed Bert. "I'll bet a dollar it was that whack on the head that's changed Ray." He turned to Ray, his tone incisive. "Don't you see? This is the first game you've played since that Springfield affair. Maybe that ball hit some nerve center—or whatever you call it and it's just made you temporarily nervous up there at the plate."

"Maybe you're right, Bert," agreed Charlie.

"I'm sure of it." Bert was emphatic. "You'll be all right in a few days, Ray. Just wait and see."

But he wasn't. And gradually his chums began to worry. Day after day in practice Ray experienced the same horrible sensation of deadly fear when he faced the slants of his teammates during batting drills. Desperation made him stay up there even though perspiration studded his cheeks and brow, and a cold dread knotted the muscles in his stomach each time a whizzing ball arced toward him.

Gradually the rest of the players began to notice it. Instead of the usually cheerful aspect of the club there was now a general air of gloom pervading the practice sessions. Strangely enough, even though Ray was a new member on the team, the players had come to look to Ray to pace them in batting. And batting in the clean-up slot, the entire attack of the Clarkville nine was built around Ray.

But Ray had failed in the Bridgeport contest and he looked miserable in the practice sessions. Finally Jimmy Ames came over to him.

"You'll have to snap out of it, Ray."

Ray gave the coach a tight, strained glance. "I'm trying to."

"It's just a slump, Coach," stated Bert loyally.

"I hope that's all it is," retorted Ames, and his sharp gaze appeared to drill right through Ray. "We need your hitting and if you can't come through I'll have to bench you."

"Of course," said Ray huskily. "I don't want to hurt the team."

And then because this terrible fear that had claimed him left him trembling with rage and something almost akin to tears, he turned his back on the coach and walked out to the field to shag flies. There was a lump in his throat as he thought grimly of his fading chances to remain on the team.

CHAPTER V

TUG-OF-WAR

RAY jumped up from the chair he had been occupying and strode to the window.

"I can't stand it any more," he said savagely and thrust his hands deeply into his trouser pockets.

Outside the ground was soggy from an all-morning rain which had influenced Jimmy Ames in cancelling baseball practice for the afternoon. Heavy clouds still moved swiftly across the gray sky but now the rain had stopped.

"Still worried about your hitting?" Tom inquired.

The entire group comprising Tom, Bert, Charlie, Ros, Jack and Ray were sprawled on beds and chairs in the wide room of Corbin Hall. Cancellation of practice had left them all with nothing to do. And none of them was in the mood for studying at the moment.

Ray whirled. "What else?"

"Don't be so jumpy," cautioned Charlie.

Ray's eyes were cloudy. "If you knew how I felt, you wouldn't talk about being jumpy. I've had my heart set on winning a permanent place on the team.

46

Just when it looks like I'm getting a break, I get beaned and suddenly I'm scared stiff at the plate. I can see it coming. I'll be benched."

"Don't think of that," said Ros.

Ray paid no heed. "No use kidding myself. I'm a hindrance to the team. I'll give myself a few more days and if I don't snap out of it, I'll quit."

The broad-shouldered lad's face was bleak. Fierce, set lines bracketed his long lips. Every boy in the room could tell by the vehemence of his talk how much remaining on the team meant to Ray, yet here he was willing to sacrifice himself for the benefit of the school.

"You can thank Bart Himber for your condition," erupted Bert, his eyes flashing with anger.

"It might have been an accident," was Jack's quiet opinion.

"Nobody will convince me of that," replied Bert tersely. "That chap was aiming them at our heads whenever he had a chance, trying to scare us away and keep us uneasy. He came too close with one of those 'dusters' and hit Ray."

Ray broke in roughly, his lips closely pressed over his teeth. "That's something I aim to find out about. For some reason Himber took a dislike to me. Maybe he did it purposely after I whacked that home run. If he did, he'll answer for it."

"We're with you on that," Bert said quickly, a fiery, belligerent gleam lighting up his eyes. "And if we meet up with that fellow, I hope he brings his pal, Fred

Dressen along. They looked like two of the same stripe to me."

"If you fellows are looking to meet Himber and Dressen you may have your chance sooner than you expect," said Tom, rising from one of the beds to pace up and down the room.

"What do you mean?" demanded Ray.

"Heck, did you forget the track meet here the day after we play Walton? It's a triangular meet between Clarkville, Walton and Springfield. There'll be a big bunch of rooters from Springfield to see that meet since it's on a Saturday afternoon and there are no classes. Don't be surprised if you see your friends here then."

"I certainly hope they come," breathed Ray, his eyes turning to chips of blue ice.

"That goes double for me," issued from the Clarkville catcher.

"This sitting around is driving me crazy," stated Ros. He, too, rose and strode to the window. For a moment he looked down on the slowly drying flagstone walks, the soaked lawns, then he pivoted to face the rest of the room. "I've got an idea!"

"If it's something to take us out of this room, let's hear it," grunted Jack Lowell, flexing his shoulder muscles in a gesture of weary impatience.

"It will," replied Ros. "After this rain there ought to be a nice big mud hole behind the gymnasium as usual. I say this is a swell time to have a tug-of-war."

Bert let out a war whoop. "That *is* an idea. Lead me to it!"

"I'm just in the mood for action," was Ray's comment.

"Sure you are," agreed Ros. "It'll help you let out some of that excess steam in your system."

"Come on!" urged Tom, rushing to the door. "We'll rustle up a good stout rope and round up a bunch from Corbin and divide the sides equally."

With a wild roar the entire group went brawling out of the room. They raced down the corridors, pounding on every door as they went.

"Everybody out for the tug-of-war!"

One door popped open and a tousled, sleep-eyed head peered into the hallway. "Where's it going to be?"

"Back of the gym!"

"Hurry up, fellows, or you'll miss the fun! All out for the tug-of-war. The losers get a free mud bath!"

In a very short time three dozen eager, shouting boys were racing across the campus toward the gymnasium and the deep depression behind the building which always filled up with muddy water after a heavy rain. Bert disappeared within the ivy-covered structure but emerged a moment later with a long strand of heavy rope.

"Here we are, fellows!" he shouted. "Let's choose up sides!"

"All right," answered another lad. "You and Tom be captains. Each pick your men."

The suggestion met with favor and Tom and Bert proceeded to choose the boys they wished to have on their side. In the course of the selection Ray found himself linked with Bert and Ros, while Jack and Charlie were picked by Tom. Finally, the selection was completed and there were eighteen boys on each team.

Bert raised his hand for silence. "We'll start about twenty feet back of this big mud puddle, and the team to pull the first six boys of the other team into the mud will become the winner. Fair enough?"

"You bet!" was the eager chorus of answers.

Ray was forgetting his somber thoughts and the prospect of fun with the added risk of being doused in mud, stirred his reckless spirit.

"Who's going to take first place on the rope?" he inquired.

Bert glanced up, saw every eye upon him and grinned. "Guess I've got to be the sucker since I'm captain." He was thinking ruefully that if the other side proved stronger, he would be the first to be dragged into the mud.

"I'll take second spot," offered Ray.

"Make me third," chimed in Ros.

And so on down the line the boys took their positions.

On the other side of the ditch Tom's crew was being similarly arranged. All hands gripped the rope tightly, stout legs braced for the first tug.

"Ready?" queried Bert.

"Ready," came Tom's quick reply.

"Then let's go!"

Both sides gave a mighty heave. Tom's line was propelled forward a few feet as Bert and Ray and the others pulled with all their strength. Then Tom's cohorts braced.

"Give them all you've got," urged Tom.

Shoulders and arms and backs went into the concerted heave of that stalwart line. Slowly but surely Bert's team found itself dragged toward the ditch.

"Hold them!" appealed Bert.

Bert and Ray and Ros were leaning far back on the rope, their heels dug in the soft turf, tugging with desperate strength. And still they were being pulled toward the mud. First they were only fifteen feet away, then ten and finally five.

Bert was getting red in the face. Perspiration was running down his ruddy cheeks as it was lacing the cheeks of every boy. Ray was gritting his teeth, the muscles in his back and arms standing out like bands of supple steel.

"We've got them going!" shouted Tom to his loyal crew. "Keep it up, gang!"

"Hold that line!" shouted Bert.

Again and again he urged the boys behind him to brace and stop their inevitable march toward the ditch.

"Save your breath, Bert," taunted Tom. "You'll need it when you hit the water."

Bert snorted and bent to the stout rope again. There was another strong heave on the hempen strand and Bert was dragged along the slippery ground. He found himself on a slight incline. The water was directly below him. Closer and closer it came. Then there was a shout of triumph from the other line as Bert sloshed into the water. Behind him Ray was dragged into the pit.

"There they go!" exulted Tom. "Just a little more, gang!"

Bert was up to his knees now and Ros had been dragged into the water. The boy behind Ros was at the edge of the water and Bert's line was wavering.

"Wait, I've got an idea," hissed Ray. "It's our only chance." Both boys were straining at the rope, digging in sharply, trying to keep from being dragged into the deeper portion of the ditch.

"Quick! Spill it!" grunted Bert, his breath gushing from his lungs in a long, ragged sigh.

Ray whispered to Bert and Bert nodded.

"I'll pass it along the line," said Ray and swung back to Ros.

For the moment the lines appeared to be at a standstill. Tom's crew could not pull Bert's side farther into the ditch, but neither could Bert's crew move themselves out of their predicament.

"Let's finish it!" called Tom shrilly. "Get ready for one big heave!"

"Stop them now!" yelled Bert in frantic haste. All down the line heads were nodding as strained, reddening faces relayed Ray's instructions to one boy after another until the anchor man was reached.

Tom's crew set themselves, leaned forward, then plunged back in a mighty effort. At that moment, Bert's cohorts suddenly slackened their hold on the rope without actually letting go of it or letting it slip through their fingers. This action propelled them forward a step or two, and two boys behind Ros found themselves floundering in mud.

"Now!" erupted Bert in strident tones.

Suddenly life seemed to surge back into that wavering line. Ray and Ros and every boy down the line bent fresh effort to their pulling. That sudden slackening in the rope threw some of Bert's charges off balance. Now, before they could right themselves, Bert's crew was hauling savagely on the rope.

Swiftly and inexorably Bert, Ray and Ros sped backward out of the ditch. They kept on moving while on the other side deep ridges were made in the springy turf as Tom's cohorts dug in their heels and were dragged along in this irresistible motion.

Ten, fifteen, twenty feet Bert's line swept backward. Then Tom and Jack and Charlie found themselves plunged in the sea of mud and water. The boys behind them were literally dragged off their feet as they, too, plunged into the ditch.

"Hurrah! We win!" shouted Bert.

"The best team always wins!" was Ray's laughing addition.

"Is that so?" demanded Tom, his hands and arms muddy. He turned and spoke to Jack and Charlie.

Suddenly Tom's crew broke from the mud and charged upon Bert's weary crew. In a flash the entire thirty-six boys were engaged in a laughing, roaring free-for-all encounter. Boys were wrestling and shoving one another all over the soggy ground. Bert locked with Tom and the two of them tripped and went rolling straight into the ditch. They staggered to their feet, dripping with muddy water and immediately resumed their tussle.

Ray had his hands full with Jack Lowell. Jack's first rush carried Ray off balance. Jack got his arms about Ray's waist and started to exert a steady pressure. Ray heaved desperately, threw his legs in a scissor grip about his chum's middle and together they toppled to the ground. Over and over they rolled, each trying for a grip. Jack got on top of Ray and tried to pin his arms down at a level with his shoulders, but Ray squirmed free and got an arm-lock about Jack's head.

Suddenly Ros and Charlie, locked in a tight struggle spilled on top of them and the holds of both boys were broken. Once again they sprang at each other. Ray found himself at the edge of the ditch and before he could stop himself, he slid into the water. A shove of

Jack's fist pushed his face under water. Ray came up, gurgling for breath, as he lunged swiftly aside. He flung out his leg and tripped Jack as the latter was scrambling to his feet.

Jack pitched on his stomach and Ray piled on top of him, rolling him head-down into the water. Then it was Jack's turn to come up gasping for air. Both boys suddenly sat back and laughed.

"Boy, that was a session!" gasped Jack.

"You're a sight," Ray told him.

"You're certainly not eligible right now to pose for a collar ad," was the laughing rejoinder.

All around them other boys had stopped struggling and were joking and shouting.

"What a workout!" breathed Bert, his hair tangled with mud, his shirt and trousers streaked and thoroughly soaked. "I'm getting hungry."

"There he goes!" laughed Tom. "My roommate wants to eat again."

"Well, I guess we all had enough," said Ray, hauling himself to his feet and shivering a trifle in the cool afternoon breeze. "And speaking of eats, the clock on the chapel says five-thirty which means we've just enough time left to clean ourselves up and get over to the refectory for supper."

Without further discussion the merry troupe raced back to Corbin Hall.

CHAPTER VI

BATTING SLUMP

Two days after the tug-of-war the Clarkville nine journeyed by bus to the southern part of the state to play its annual game with Walton Academy. Although this contest was supposed to be just a "breather" on the Light and Dark Blue schedule, Coach Jimmy Ames was considerably worried about the outcome.

Five minutes before game-time Ames gathered his tense charges about him in a tight circle.

"Attention, everyone!" snapped Ames. His eyes were deadly serious and studied each boy with a deliberate and careful scrutiny. "I want you fellows to go out on the field and grab this game quickly! You've all been listless this past week. I know there were a couple of bad days when we couldn't practice, but even that shouldn't slow you fellows down.

"Yesterday you looked worse than at any time this season. Half of you aren't hitting. And that goes for you, Ray—I've been waiting for you to snap out of your slump. Don't be so tight up at the plate. Loosen up. All of you make up your minds that you must play heads-up ball all the way.

"Some of you expect this game to be easy. Well, it should be. But it's not won yet. You'll have to hit and you'll have to field better than you've been doing if you expect to beat Walton. All right, that's all. Just remember, it's your game. Whether Clarkville wins or loses depends on you fellows who are playing!"

There was a shrill call from the umpire, a yell from the Walton rooting section and the home squad raced out on the diamond to take up their positions.

"Look's like we're all on the pan," observed Ros to Ray and Bert as they moved off toward the visitors' bench with the rest of the Light and Dark Blue nine.

"Ames looked quite upset," said Bert.

"Heck, my poor playing has been catching, I guess," stated Ray.

"Don't be silly," protested lanky Tom Raynor with a grin.

"I'm disgusted. I can't seem to do a thing," said Ray. "I'm not hitting. I'm scared stiff up at the plate, and to top it off I've been missing balls in the outfield that I'd ordinarily catch with my eyes closed."

Ros gave Ray a playful dig in the ribs. "Don't be a gloomy Gus. We're all pressing too much. Once we loosen up and start to play naturally we'll be all right."

"Let's hope so," grunted Jack Lowell.

Suddenly the game got under way. Charlie Minor struck at the first ball and bounced it right back to the pitcher. The latter scooped it up and tossed it easily to the first baseman for the initial out. Bob Banks could do no better and was retired on a grounder. Ros, however, managed to pick out a pitch to his liking, punching it into center field for a base knock.

Ray strode to the plate amid the fervent cheers of his teammates and proceeded to strike out on four pitches. It was with a heavy heart and drooping shoulders that Ray took his station in left field. He had looked miserable at bat. The old fear was still with him. It was like a horrible plague, a clinging pestilence, eating away at the inner fibres of his being. Although Ros had said nothing, he imagined that the other lad had regarded him with a slow stare of disappointment.

Ray had to face it. He was a failure in the eyes of his friends and fellow athletes. He was a detriment to the Clarkville nine.

Three innings went by with neither team having any success in pushing runs across the platter. In that time Walton failed to get a man to first as Tom turned back each batter to face him. Clarkville had made no threatening gestures after Ros' opening inning single.

In the fourth frame Bob Banks led off with a walk. Ros tried hard to advance him to second on a hit-and-run play but only succeeded in forcing Bob at the keystone sack. Then with one strike against Ray, Ros elected to steal and managed to beat the Walton backstop's heave by an eyelash. Thus, Clarkville had a runner in scoring position. Any kind of safe hit should produce a tally.

With perspiration studding his brow, every muscle taut, every nerve screaming with cold fear, Ray faced the Walton moundsman. He let a wide one go by for a ball. Then the pitcher came through with a fast one, high and inside. Terror drove Ray backward, cowering away from the curving pellet which slid down over the inside corner for a strike. Finally, Ray lashed desperately at another inside pitch and sent a dribbler straight back at the Walton hurler.

The pitcher swooped down on the trickling baseball, whirled and whipped it to the third baseman. Ros was caught in a run-down between second and third and, though he made a valiant effort to out-race the gauntlet he was tagged near third. Ray went down to second on the play but perished there while Jack Lowell flied out to deep right field.

Ray risked a glance toward the Clarkville bench. He shuddered at sight of Coach Ames striding up and down along the foul line. The Clarkville coach shook his head in a gesture of mingled anger and despair. Once again the Light and Dark Blue had failed to come through in a pinch.

Walton, however, brought the spectators to their feet pleading for runs when the first batter drove a clean hit between first and second. Tom worked carefully on the next hitter and brought the count to two-and-two. Then Bert called for an outcurve. Tom complied but the pitch failed to break properly, and the batter slammed it between Bob Banks and Bill Prudy for another safety.

Ray charged in on the bounding ball, intent on keeping the runner on first from reaching third. He came in fast, put his glove down then gasped in dismay when the ball skidded through his legs. He whirled and chased after it. As he retrieved it, he saw that the boy who had been on first was about to score, so he whipped it to Bob but not in time to nail the batter who came to rest at the hot corner in a cloud of dust.

Ray groaned. A two-base error! One run in, a runner on third and no one out. He jogged back to his position, pounded his glove angrily with a knotted fist and waited for the next play.

"Too bad, Ray!" sang out Ros. "Don't worry. We'll get the next three. One run is Walton's limit."

Ray smiled weakly. There was no laughter in him at the moment. Only despair and fuming anger with himself. The crack of bat meeting ball jolted him out of his somber reflections. He saw a gleaming white sphere zooming toward him. He turned and raced back fifteen feet to spear the ball. Regaining his balance, he noted how the Walton runner tagged up at third and sprinted for home.

His lips grim and determined, eyes flashing, Ray sent the ball rocketing toward Bert. Again he groaned when he saw the ball curve to the left of the plate. It pulled Bert out of the base path and though the Clarkville catcher caught it with his bare right hand and left his feet in a frantic lunge to tag the runner, the Walton player slid safely home under his outstretched arm.

A roar of approval came from the Walton rooters.

"Come on, gang!" was the fervent cry. "We've got Clarkville on the run!"

"Knock Raynor out of the box!"

"Hit them to the left fielder! He can't catch 'em!"

This last strident call cut deep into Ray's feelings. He was directly responsible for both of Walton's tallies. Both were the result of his slip-shod playing. And this sloppy defense work seemed to communicate itself to Bill Prudy at short when the latter muffed an easy chance of a grounder a moment later.

Further trouble was averted, however, when Tom turned on the heat and whiffed the next two batters. Coming off the field and marching over to the Clarkville bench, Ray glanced expectantly toward Ames. He was prepared for a thorough "dressing down," or severe reprimand for the two miscues he had made in left field, but Ames did not even glance in his direction.

In fact, the Clarkville mentor said nothing to his players. He had no instructions for Bert West who was slated to lead off for the Light and Dark Blue. There was no change in the somber expression on his cheeks when Bert laced a clean single into short left center. Only the lines about his mouth appeared to tighten when Bill Prudy fanned. They became more pronounced when Pete Smith was retired on a grounder, Bert going to second on the play. Once again a Clarkville threat was extinguished when the Walton pitcher induced Tom to pop to the third baseman.

Charlie Minor dropped a throw from Bill Prudy to put the first batter on base at the beginning of Walton's half of the fifth. Once more Tom was required to tighten up. By dint of careful pitching to "spots," he forced the second batter to bounce into a double play, and when the third player lifted a high fly to Charlie, the inning was over.

In the sixth Charlie Minor tried to work the Walton flinger for a base on balls, but was fooled by a change-of-pace pitch and was called out on strikes. Bob Banks couldn't do any better than lining one right into the hands of the Walton second sacker.

Ros followed Bob with a hard-hit grounder to deep short. The Walton fielder succeeded in knocking the ball down but could not retrieve it in time to toss Ros out. It was scored as a hit.

Then it was Ray's turn. He trudged to the plate with fear tugging at the ragged edges of his nerves. He was torn by a terrible dread of being struck by a ball and by a fear that was almost as great—fear of again failing in the pinch.

The Walton pitcher took a short wind-up, rocked back on his heels and poured in a fast one, high and inside. Ray ducked back awkwardly. An Arctic wind seemed to be racing up and down his spine. The next pitch was low and outside. Then came a hummer right down the middle for a called strike.

Ray set himself, instinctively expecting a fast one, inside. He ground his teeth together to keep them from chattering. His scalp actually seemed to crawl with terror. It was as if he waited for the shock of seamed horsehide colliding with his head.

There was a flash of white out on the mound. The ball winged toward the plate, twirling end over end, then dipping and curving inside. Ray lunged backward, twisting aside in a half crouch. In avoiding the throw, Ray's bat completed a quarter arc and met the ball obliquely, popping it out into short right field.

The first and second baseman scampered out from their positions, trying to outrace the flight of the ball. In from right field charged the right fielder. For a moment it appeared that the three players would collide. Then, they halted and the ball dropped safely between them while Ray was racing for first, rounding the sack and legging it for second.

Ros had hesitated halfway between first and second, fearing that the ball might be caught. As it dropped safely between the fielders he, too, put on the steam and streaked past second and made third standing up. Ray was forced to slide but managed to beat the right fielder's hurried throw.

Now it was Clarkville's turn to cheer. There were runners on second and third with two out and Jack Lowell coming up to hit.

"Get a hit, Jack!" called Ros from third.

"Save me a lick!" implored Bert, resting on one knee near the plate, bat fisted and ready to trudge to the plate should Jack get on base.

"I'll do my best," promised Jack.

And he did. He lashed out at the first pitch and drove a savage grounder past the Walton hurler. The latter flung his gloved hand at the racing ball and came up with thin air. The second baseman bolted to the keystone sack and made a great one-handed stop of the ball, then pivoted to whip it to first. But Jack, running like the wind, beat the throw.

In the meantime Ros and Ray were burning up the sod in a mad dash around the bases. Both boys broke with the pitch and Ros was three-quarters of the way home by the time Jack hit the ball. Ros scored easily. Ray, seeing how deeply the ball had been hit, decided on a daring attempt to score also. His move was altogether unexpected. The Walton catcher had taken a few paces forward to put himself in front of the plate. Now he screamed frantically for the ball.

Legs driving like great pistons, Ray pounded down the base line. He saw in a white blur how the Walton initial sacker whirled, a look of amazement on his features, then cocked his arm back to throw it to the catcher. Ray was halfway down the line, then three-quarters when he saw the backstop station himself squarely in the base path.

There was the smack of a ball plunking into a mitt as Ray hurled his body forward in a long hook slide. Ray's rugged frame shuddered with the terrific impact as he and the catcher collided. Ray slid under the catcher. A cloud of dust rose to cloak both boys. Ray felt the ball touch his arm, then the breath was torn from his lungs as he knocked the catcher from his feet and both boys rolled in the turf.

"Safe!"

For a moment neither boy could move. Ray opened his eyes with a painful effort and saw the ball a few feet away from him. Beside him the catcher was dragging himself to his knees.

"Boy, you hit me like a ten-ton truck," the Walton player grunted.

"Sorry, I had to," murmured Ray. "You were blocking the base line."

Someone hauled Ray to his feet. A hand pounded his back. It was Bert.

"Good boy! That was base running. Ties up the old ball game!"

CHAPTER VII

BENCHED FOR WEAK HITTING

RAY returned to the Clarkville bench, glancing hopefully at Jimmy Ames, but the latter was staring moodily across the sun-dappled diamond. It occurred to Ray, then, in a dismal sense of reality that his base hit had been decidedly tainted and he therefore deserved no praise.

Thus, he sat gloomily watching the Walton hurler regain his poise to set down the Light and Dark Blue batters without further scoring. Walton could do nothing with Tom's slants in the latter half of the sixth and the game rolled on past the seventh and eighth with the score still tied at 2–2.

In the ninth it was Ray's turn to lead off for Clarkville. This time the Walton hurler took no chances with Ray. Evidently he had received strict instructions from the catcher to keep them high and inside, and he had Ray cringing in stark terror again as ball after ball drove him away from the plate.

Ray's nerves were taut and he felt like screaming. It required a desperate effort of his will to remain at the plate. Each pitch was a fresh torment. The blood seemed to drain from his body and his ears began to ring. At last, as if from a great distance, he heard the umpire call him out on strikes and wave him toward the bench.

Then Jimmy Ames lost his control. As Ray trudged despondently toward his teammates, Ames leaped to his feet.

"Great guns, Ray! What *is* the matter with you? You looked like a wooden Indian up there. Swing at the ball as if you really meant to hit it. Anyone watching you would think you were scared." Ames stopped and his glance raked Ray severely. "Are you?"

The question hit Ray with the shock of a bullet. It staggered him, set him back a pace. Crimson spots of color flooded his cheeks.

"No—no, coach," he said huskily. "It isn't that. It's—"

"Never mind now," snapped Ames. "We've got to win this game and we'll never win it this way." He looked up, his jaw rigidly set, as Jack Lowell beat out an infielder roller for a hit. He gripped Bert's arm as the latter was about to move toward the plate. "No bunting. Hit it out, Bert."

"I'll sure try," grunted Bert.

Bert waited carefully while the Walton pitcher spun two strikes and two balls past him. Then he found a toss to his liking and hammered it out to center field for a single, Jack scooting around to third on the hit.

Ames then decided on a little strategy. With only a long fly needed to bring in a run, the Clarkville coach instructed Prudy to lay down a bunt between first and the pitcher's box. It was Ames' idea that Walton would never be expecting such tactics.

Accordingly, Prudy waved his bat menacingly at the Walton moundsmen. He gripped the willow down near the handle. The ball left the hurler's hand. Swiftly Prudy slid his hands up along the bat and brought it lightly against the whistling sphere. The ball dropped, spinning and twisting crazily near the first base line. The play took Walton by surprise.

Jack was halfway home before the Walton pitcher started moving for the elusive trickler, and by the time the ball was recovered there was no chance for a play at home. Jack scored easily. In fact, by fast running Prudy almost beat the delayed throw to first.

Clarkville was unable to add any more tallies that inning, but that one run proved sufficient margin for victory, since Tom retired Walton in order in the last half of the ninth. As for Ray, he received an inkling of Ames' feelings toward him when the Clarkville coach sent Al Larson out to left field to take his place for the half inning. Ray realized with a qualm of fear and despair that this action was equivalent to telling Ray that he had been cut off the squad.

This suspicion was confirmed a little later when Ames

stalked into the dressing room and gave his charges a verbal lashing that they all long remembered. He minced no words, reminding them that their victory over Walton was a lucky one. The breaks had gone their way, but once they went to the opposition Clarkville would be finished.

Afterward, Ames directed his attention to individual players, picking out flaws in their play.

"I can't understand what's come over you. You're all jittery as if this was the first game of the season. For some of you, this is your third year on the squad, but to look at you out on the Walton diamond you would never know it." Ames' voice had a thin, cutting quality to it.

"Ray," said Ames suddenly, regret showing on his weathered cheeks, "you're not the same ball player you were two weeks ago. Sometimes I think you're dreaming or are worried about something. I'm sorry to say that until you show definite improvement, I'll have to use Al Larson in left field."

Ray nodded silently. His heart was too full with remorse and shame to talk. He felt the inquisitive eyes of some of his teammates upon him and had to turn his head away. Over the heads of some of the players, he saw Bert looking at him. There was sympathy in the stocky lad's eyes. He gestured toward Ames and his lips formed a soundless sentence.

Ray understood by this silent entreaty that Bert was

urging him to explain to Ames this strange fear that gripped him when he was up at the plate. But this was something he could not speak about to the coach. He had his pride and he could not ask for sympathy. And so his mouth folded in a tight gesture of negation. He lifted his eyes suddenly and snapped to attention when Ames resumed talking.

"I've been holding off some good news for you chaps, waiting for a good time to spring it. I was hoping that Clarkville would look good today, look like the champion it should be, but I regret to say that this has not been the case.

"However, I can't very well delay telling you that the State Scholastic Baseball league has decided to sponsor an all-star team this Spring."

"An all-star team!" repeated Bert. "Boy, that sounds great!"

"I'm not so sure that it is—for us," responded Ames quietly.

"But what's it all about?" demanded Bill Prudy.

"The details are by no means complete," remarked Ames, "but for the present it has been decided that directly before the last game of the season a team of scholastic all-stars will be selected. All selections are to be based strictly on performance in inter-scholastic games. The boys lucky enough to make the squad will make a trip to Cuba to play a similar team of all-stars selected from school nines on the island."

"Cuba! Did you hear that, gang?" demanded Bert. He let out a wild yell.

"Whoopee!" sang out a chorus of eager voices.

"Cuba, here we come!"

Me for the tropics!" shouted Pete Smith.

Ames lifted his hand for silence. "None of you will reach Cuba on the basis of this afternoon's play. Just bear that in mind."

"By the way, Mr. Ames, who will do the picking?" queried Tom.

"The coaches of the various school teams. No coach will be permitted to vote for players on his own team. In that manner, we all feel the selections will be impartial and made truly on the basis of merit."

"Would I like to make that trip!" breathed Ros. "That trip down to Florida last year with the football squad to play in the Orange Bowl spoiled me. I've got a hankering for warm climates."

Once again Ames signalled for silence. "All right, fellows, that's all. Take your showers and change into your clothes. Our bus leaves in forty minutes and I want you all ready in time. Seriously, every one of you will have to buckle down and work hard. I'd like to see several of you make the team."

"But if any of us are picked, would Dr. Holbrook permit us to go?" demanded Jack Lowell.

"I've already discussed that with Dr. Holbrook and his answer was yes."

"Well, that's one thing settled."

"Sure," said Bert with a grin. "The next thing is to make the all-star team."

Forty minutes later the special bus which had brought the Clarkville aggregation to Walton was rolling along a smooth concrete highway, headed for home. Ray, Tom, Bert and the rest of their friendly clan took refuge in the rear of the swaying vehicle. There was plenty of conversation, and most of it centered around the all-star team and each individual's chances for making the coveted trip to Cuba.

"That's the best news I've heard since Dr. Holbrook announced in the refectory last Fall that Clarkville had been invited to play in the Orange Bowl in Miami on New Year's Eve for the National Scholastic Football Championship against the Tampico eleven." Ros was jubilant and his cheeks were flushed with pleasure. He nudged Ray. "Well, say something. Don't you think so?"

There was a hurt bewilderment in Ray's eyes when he met his chum's smiling gaze. "Sure, it's swell news. But what good will it do me when I'm off the team?"

"Ames won't keep you off long," assured Bert loyally. "Once you snap out of your slump you'll be whaling that old apple over all the fences again."

"I may never come out of the slump—as you call it."

Ros cut in sharply. "What you need, Ray, is another whack on the head to make you normal again."

Ray stiffened. Knotted muscles rode the lean line of

his jaw. He was silent for several seconds while he considered what Ros had said. "Maybe you're right," he murmured quietly, his chin lifting in a strange gesture of determination.

Ros laughed. "Don't take me seriously. I don't want you ramming that skull of yours into every door you see."

"I won't ram it into any doors," promised Ray.

There was something in his tone which hinted at thoughts left unexpressed. Ros regarded him soberly and appeared to be ready to question Ray when Bert interrupted the trend of his reflections.

"Here's one chap that's buckling down to serious baseball from now on," affirmed the Clarkville catcher. "I think I need an ocean voyage for my health." He ducked instinctively as Tom swung the palm of his hand over his head.

"What you need more than anything else," stated Tom, "is to go on a strict diet of bread and water for several weeks in order to remove some of that fat from your waddling frame."

Bert pretended offense. "I'll have you know I've got quite a nice shape."

"Sure," said Ray, forgetting for the moment his somber mood, "if anyone could see you in a bathing suit they'd take that round middle of yours for a pair of rubber tires."

In a moment Bert had let out a roar and leaped upon Ray. They wrestled around in the back of the bus,

threshing across the swaying floor, pummeling one another good-naturedly until finally a sudden lurch of the
vehicle sent them both careening into Tom's lap. Immediately Ros and Jack and Charlie Minor swooped in
to subdue the struggling pair and restore order.

CHAPTER VIII

A MEETING WITH HIMBER

RAY HENNESSEY raced down the steps of Corbin Hall on the following Saturday afternoon and halted beside a blooming lilac bush. He turned to look back toward the doorway.

"Bert! Tom! Ros! Hurry up or we'll miss the first few events in the track meet."

Already a steady line of Clarkville students were marching toward Alumni Field where the triangular meet between Clarkville, Springfield and Walton was to be staged. On the program was a large list of sprints, one and two-mile runs, a five-mile cross-country race, pole vaulting, broad jumping, high jumping, and low and high hurdle races.

At last Bert and Tom and Ros appeared. Charlie and Jack were not with them because both boys were on the track team and were entered in the sprints.

"Thought you fellows would never come," said Ray.

"Can't you guess what kept us?" inquired Tom. He gestured toward Bert.

Ray glanced at the stocky lad, noted how his right cheek was distended by something he was chewing.

"Holy smoke! Don't you ever get tired of eating?"

Bert grinned calmly. "Never." Then he glanced curiously at Ray. "You're mighty interested in getting over there. Never knew you to show such an interest in track before."

"It ought to be a good meet," said Ray glibly.

"You wouldn't be counting on seeing our friends Bart Himber and Fred Dressen from Springfield, would you?"

Ray smiled but the gesture was made only with his lips. His eyes were suddenly hard and dangerous. "I wouldn't walk out of the way to avoid them."

"And neither would I!" grunted Bert, all pleasantness whipping out of his ruddy cheeks.

Together the four chums moved across the campus. Occasionally they espied friends and called jovial greetings to them. They were nearing Alumni Field when a streamlined bus, carrying a huge Springfield banner along its painted side, skidded to a stop near the parking lot beside the field.

Instinctively Ray halted to watch the shouting group of boys who tumbled from the bus and scampered toward the quickly filling stands.

"There they are!" grated Ray.

The harsh sound of his voice jerked his chums around. They, too, had stopped to regard the new arrivals. Now their eyes followed Ray's gaze and picked out the strong, rangy shapes of Himber and Dressen.

It was almost as if some quality in Ray's fierce glance

had the power to attract the object of his penetrating attention.   For, suddenly the two Springfield lads turned toward the four Clarkville students and their expression darkened.   Himber said something to Dressen.   The latter glanced toward Alumni Field, nodded tersely, and together the two boys changed their direction and approached Ray and his friends.

"Here it comes," said Bert tensely.

"If you mean trouble," observed Tom shrewdly, "I'd say you were dead right."

"Bert doesn't mean anything else," snapped Ray. He spoke in a deadly voice—a voice which somehow held back a furious, wild emotion.   "I've been looking forward to this meeting."

"Looks like they've been looking forward to it, too," was Ros' terse comment.

All four Clarkville boys noted the savage pleasure which pulled at the rugged features of the Springfield ball players.   There was a confident, arrogant swagger to their stride.   They stopped a few feet away from Ray and his chums and Himber's mouth twisted in a sneer.

"Well, if it isn't Clarkville's great slugger!"

"You trying to be wise?" demanded Bert sharply, his face darkening.

Ray broke in swiftly.   "Let me handle this, Bert."

"Handle what?" snapped Himber.   His shoulders stirred idly and his dark eyes burned with a fierce light.

"I'm coming to that," murmured Ray, an ominous

softness in his tone. He was a rigid shape before the bigger Springfield lad. There was no cringe in him, no fear. He might have a dread of a horneting baseball when he was up at the plate, but he knew no fear of this arrogant boy who faced him. "I owe you something for those 'dusters' you were tossing against us a couple of weeks ago."

"Dusters!" Himber pretended surprise. He turned to Dressen. "Did you hear that, Fred? I'm beginning to think that talk about these Clarkville chaps being a bunch of sissies is correct. They're afraid of a ball that comes a little too close to them."

"Watch your talk," warned Ray.

"We'll watch nothing," responded Dressen tartly.

"I'm convinced you were deliberately throwing bean balls," said Ray doggedly. His lips were a grim, solid line against his taut features. "You might have killed one of us and you did hit me."

Himber laughed. It was not a pleasant sound to hear. "Yeah, we've been hearing things about you. Seems Clarkville's great home run ace is afraid of his shadow. They say he can't hit the side of a barn. All because he's gone yellow!"

"You bought trouble when you said that, Himber," Ray informed the Springfield pitcher quietly. He spoke in a voice so gentle it held infinite menace.

For a moment Himber appeared to be disturbed, and his eyes raked Ray with an unrelenting tension. Then

a surly, arrogant grin crept across his features, turning them definitely unpleasant.

"He's throwing a bluff, Bart," broke in Fred Dressen
with a snort of derision.

"In a second you're going to find out just how much
he's bluffing," warned Bert loyally, angry blood stain-
ing his cheeks.

"Keep your oar out of this, fat-stuff," mocked Dressen, "or you'll get your face pushed in."

Ray glanced at Bert and their eyes locked in mute
agreement. Bert nodded, pressure flowing through all
his muscles. Vibrations of rage were thrumming
through Ray, girding him for explosive action. He
took a step toward Himber, purpose written in grim
lines all over his face.

"What are we waiting for?"

"You said it, Ray," intoned Bert. "No time like the
present for putting these birds in their place."

Himber and Dressen straightened. They were big,
husky boys. They towered over Ray and Bert and
they anticipated with a certain wicked pleasure the encounter that was sure to take place.

"I'm going to enjoy giving you a hiding, Hennessey," stated Himber boldly.

"Just make sure your pals don't butt into this argu-
ment," grunted Dressen as he pivoted to face Bert
squarely. He shot a glance at Tom and Ros who were
grim and interested spectators.

"We won't be needing any help, my friend," murmured Ray to Fred Dressen and stepped swiftly toward Bart Himber.

Ray's piston-like left rammed the side of the big fellow's jaw and knocked him off balance. Himber snarled, then grunted when Ray followed up his advantage with another stiff jab to the mouth. Beside the rival fighters Bert and Fred were suddenly going at it, their blows thudding heavily against one another.

"Go to it, Ray, and teach him a lesson," urged Ros, intently watching the fray.

Other boys attracted by the noise and by the sight of the four boys squaring off against each other, hurried to the scene. In a short time they were ringed in by eager faces.

Ray, anxious to keep on the offensive, rushed in again and was wild with a right. Instantly Himber stopped his backward march, straightened up and laced Ray with a torrid left under the heart. The blow brought a gasp from the Clarkville lad. He dropped his guard for a moment and Himber, noting the opening, pumped a right cross to the side of Ray's head.

Lights began to swim in front of Ray's eyes. He was amazed at the power behind the Springfield hurler's punch. The blow had shaken him up considerably. Warily he covered up while Himber lashed him savagely with both fists, trying to penetrate his defense and get in a telling blow.

A smashing right caught Ray flush on the chin and he toppled backward, landing full on his back.

"Got enough?" panted Himber, his face flushed, a fierce light glittering in his eyes.

Ray shook his head to clear it. "Not yet, friend," he said and got to his feet.

Himber rushed in swiftly, planted a hard left on Ray's right cheek, then another left to the eye and still another blow to the same place without a return. Ray staggered, blinded by the savagery of this attack.

"How do you like it, Hennessey?" grunted Himber and sent Ray reeling to the ground with a screaming right to the side of the jaw.

Pain slugged through Ray in scorching streams. He felt the energy sifting from his frame, but the sight of the leering and triumphant face above him propelled him to his feet again.

Himber didn't wait for Ray to gain his balance. Again his welt-knuckled fists lashed out, connected with flesh and bone, and spun Ray against the bole of a maple tree. A trickle of blood appeared at the corner of Ray's mouth. His hair fell across his face which had turned granite-hard. There was no mercy in his eyes now.

He hit the tree trunk with his shoulder blades and bounced straight back against the Springfield lad. Somehow he moved his head aside while a whistling right sped past his ear. Viciously Ray shot a terrific left to Himber's middle. The latter grunted, doubled up in sudden pain. A split second later Himber's head was snapped backward when a straight right cross exploded on his chin.

Desperately Himber flailed his arms, surging forward in wild rage, attempting to overwhelm Ray with the sheer force of his drive. But now Ray was fighting coolly. His chin was set, his eyes were hard and his cheeks were strict and smooth with a cold fury. He parted Himber's blows, parrying them on his arms, and slipped short sharp blows inside Himber's feeble guard.

Again and again Ray landed with telling force. A jolting uppercut made Himber tremble like a windblown pine in the face of a wilderness gale. Pressing forward with relentless fury, Ray hammered the big fellow's mid-section. Right and left, those pumping fists were sapping the strength and stamina of the Springfield pitcher. The sting evaporated from Himber's punches.

A hard fist crashed against the side of Ray's jaw but he hardly felt it. Blazing heat drove him on. A strange, turbulent wildness set his veins on fire. Nothing could have stopped him at this moment.

He saw Himber's leering, pain-wracked face and stepped boldly forward. He jabbed Himber in the mouth. Again he shot that swift flicking left, raking the Springfield lad's eyes, mouth and nose. Suddenly Himber surged forward. His arm lashed out in a wild arc. Hot pain seemed to consume Ray's body below the belt. Himber had fouled him. Again the Springfield lad's fist found that deadly mark, hitting him low, crippling him with pain.

Ray backed up, his eyes glazed. Himber was glowering with sly triumph. He rushed in, arms pumping madly, desperately. Somehow Ray blocked those savage, deadly punches, while he struggled to regain his senses. Those low blows had taken the starch out of him. His knees felt weak and he knew he wasn't far from a state of collapse.

"You coward!" Ray gritted. "You aren't man enough to fight fair."

"What's the matter? Yellow?" taunted Himber, paying no heed to Ray's charge of unfairness.

The taunt shook Ray up. His eyes narrowed and his lips set in a firm line that resembled a band of iron.

"Yellow, am I?" he whispered and stopped Himber in his tracks with a torrid left to the ribs. "I'll finish you for that."

Again Himber tried to hit Ray low, but the Clarkville lad blocked the punch. Ray countered swiftly with a savage left under the heart. Then he crossed his right to the same spot and shot a jab to Himber's jaw. He saw the Springfield boy falter and a look of growing fear crept into Himber's face.

There was a hiss of driven breath as Ray spun Himber half around with a short right. Himber lunged forward in one last desperate motion. His right fist grazed Ray's cheek. He was still off balance when Ray's left tagged his middle, and was followed in almost the same breath by a solid right that carried all of Ray's weight behind it.

Knuckles smashed against rock-hard jaw. The shock of the punch raced up Ray's arm. It set his shoulders and back a-tingle. Himber's mouth flipped open. A glazed look came into his eyes and he pitched forward on his face. He groaned, stirred feebly and then lay still.

Ray wiped blood from his mouth with his shirt sleeve and turned to watch Bert and Fred Dressen battling savagely. They were evenly matched. Both boys bore bruises from the gruelling encounter. As Ray watched, he saw Bert and Fred stand toe to toe and slug furiously. It seemed they would never stop. Both lads were giving and taking considerable punishment. But it was Dressen who finally gave ground, retreating before the lashing fury of Bert's attack.

The stout lad was winded. His breath issued from his throat in sharp, audible gasps but still he continued punching. Dressen could not keep up his guard. Bert's solid blows were crashing against his body and face. Bert tagged him with a terrific right to the jaw. The blow staggered Dressen, sent him reeling backward. He stumbled over a fallen tree branch and measured his length on the ground.

Bert stood over him. "Got enough?"

Dressen nodded miserably, his eyes like black coals, hard and unforgiving.

"Good boy, Bert," said Ray, grinning. "They both got what they were looking for." He shifted his glance to Himber. "Get up on your feet and clear out of here. The next time you feel like beaning somebody with a baseball, you'd better pick on someone you can handle."

Himber glowered darkly and rose stiffly. He put a grimed fist to his right eye which was swollen and appeared to be on the verge of closing.

"I'll get even with you for this, Hennessey," he promised.

Ray's eyebrows lifted a notch and he was very cool with his talk. "Anytime you're looking for trouble, just pay me a visit. I'll be glad to accommodate you."

"And I'll say the same for you, Dressen," warned Bert as the Springfield catcher also rose and joined his chum.

Dressen appeared to be forming an angry retort on his lips when Himber clutched his arm and spoke urgently.

"Come on, Fred. Let's get out of here. We'll see these chaps again and when we do it may be a different story."

Ray answered that cheerfully. "Sure, it may be a different story but I can promise you it'll have the same ending."

Himber's rangy body trembled under the lash of his rising temper but he said nothing. Abruptly, he and

Dressen turned their backs on the Clarkville contingent and started walking at a rapid pace away from Alumni Field.

Ros, laughing heartily, joined Ray and Bert.

"Looks like those fellows lost all interest in the track meet."

"Do you blame them?" inquired Tom. He gave Bert a slap on the back. "Bert, you're quite a scrapper. I'm thinking seriously of making a professional fighter out of you. All you need is about one hundred miles of road work to remove that rubber tire around your belt—"

Tom never finished the sentence because he was too busy racing across the campus with Bert close upon his heels and intent on playful revenge.

Ray watched the merry chase and despite his somber thoughts, he was obliged to join Ros in a peal of hearty laughter. Finally Bert caught up to Tom and the two roommates tussled roughly on the grass, slapping and cuffing one another until they were breathless.

"Didn't think you could handle your fists the way you did," Ros told Ray, admiration warming his tone.

Ray gave his chum a small smile. He rubbed the palm of his left hand across the skinned knuckles of his right hand.

"I feel a lot better now, Ros."

"Sure you do. You got a lot of poison out of your system by licking Himber."

"He's a bad number and he had it coming to him."

Ros nodded. "Something tells me you haven't heard the last of him."

"I'm not worried."

"If Springfield and Clarkville both go undefeated you'll be facing him on the diamond again in the special play-off Coach Ames was talking about."

Ray's face clouded suddenly. He was remembering his slump—the terrible vise of fear that governed his actions at the plate. He groaned as he thought of the humiliation he would suffer if he failed to hit against Himber, should they meet again. Then another thought assailed him. What if he didn't even get to play in any more games during the season?

CHAPTER IX

VICTORY FOR RAY

RAY's gloomy reflections were terminated by the arrival of Tom and Bert, both flushed from their friendly encounter. They exchanged some light banter, then hurried to Alumni Field. The stands were filled but they managed to find seats in the last row.

Although they remained until the meet was over, they were forced to admit later that they hadn't paid strict attention to the various events on the program. They did remember portions of the sprints, the high hurdle races and the pole vault contest and they knew that Springfield finally took top honors for the day, but they were very hazy about the minute details. And the reason for this was that they were occupied with discussing the fight Ray and Bert had had with Himber and Dressen, together with the prospects of meeting the two Springfield boys again, either on or off the diamond.

Two days later Ray, Bert, Tom and the others of the merry clique from Corbin Hall, hurried through their classes to repair to Alumni Field for the scheduled game with Glendale Academy. The boys changed into their playing togs quickly and raced out to the diamond to get in some early practice before the visiting nine arrived.

The coach spent a quarter hour batting fungos to Ray, Ros, Jack and the utility outfielders, while the infield was having a brisk practice of its own. At last, the Glendale squad arrived and Clarkville relinquished the diamond to the visitors. Coming off the field, Ray approached Ames.

"Coach, is there any chance of my playing today?" he asked, already dreading the answer.

Ames gave Ray a long, steady glance. "Sorry, Ray. Not today."

Ray turned away before the Clarkville coach could say anything more. There was bitterness in his heart as he watched the lively antics of the Glendale players. They were laughing and shouting to one another. Even on the Clarkville bench Ros and Tom and the others were in earnest conversation, talking about the gang. Though Ros caught his eye and gestured for him to come over, Ray already felt himself an outsider—an outcast from the team.

"All right, fellows!" snapped Ames a few moments later. "Get out there for your last practice. Everybody take five swings at the plate and let the next man bat."

Al Larson was lobbing balls in to Bert West crouching behind the plate. Soon one after the other of the Light and Dark Blue diamond stars strode to the plate and started hitting. Ray awaited his turn with that old feeling of dread.

"Over the fence, Ray. Plaster it!" whispered Ros as he finished his swings.

"Wouldn't I like to do that," groaned Ray and took his stance, facing Larson.

The first ball came in fast and was high and inside. Although Ray set his teeth firmly, resolved not to back away, still some deeper urge within him propelled him backward and away from the plate. There was a cool breeze scouring across the field yet he was perspiring freely.

"Swing at them, Ray!" called out Ames impatiently. "We haven't got all day."

Ray nodded mutely and swung awkwardly at the next pitch, popping it weakly to Charlie Minor at first base. Larson took a short wind-up and flung a half-speed ball toward the plate.

Plagued by visions of what his life on the team would be if he continued to be chained down by his fear of being beaned again, Ray decided on a desperate move. And only desperation, produced by bitter despair and intense longing to be on the team again, could have prompted him to leap forward as the gleaming white sphere swerved high and inside.

He could have swung and laced the ball over third base. Instead, he ducked his head, taking a half step across the plate without lifting the bat from his shoul-

der. The next moment there was a dull thud as the ball
struck him on the temple.

Ros and Bert shouted in dismay. A red haze of pain
funneled over Ray's brain. He swayed dizzily and collapsed in front of the plate, while the ball bounded past
Bert who paid it no heed, stripping off his mask to rush
to Ray's side.

"It's Ray! He's been hit again!" someone yelled.

"Good gosh! That's the second time!" grunted Pete
Smith and left his position at second base to join the
tense throng grouped around Ray.

"Ray! Ray! Are you all right?" Bert was shouting.

Ames pushed his way through the tight crowd. "Get
back, boys! Give him some air."

Suddenly Ray stirred and opened his eyes. His head
throbbed with pain, and for a moment all these eager
faces grouped so near him appeared to be whirling
around in circles. Then he grinned.

"Somebody run and get Doc Halsey," snapped
Ames.

"No!" protested Ray feebly. "I'm all right."

"But you've been hit on the head again," said Ames.
"Can't risk a serious injury."

"Gosh, if I didn't know you better," said Bert, "I'd
say you deliberately ran into that pitch of Al's."

"Maybe I did. Who can tell," said Ray and winked
at Ros who glanced at him in mingled bewilderment and

dismay. "Let me up. I've still got three more swings coming to me."

"Three more swings!" repeated Ames incredulously. "Boy, are you mad? I can't let you up there to bat. You're going to the infirmary for an examination."

Ray look dismayed. He had risen and with Bert and Ros half supporting him he flung his frenzied appeal at the Clarkville mentor.

"Coach, you've got to let me try to hit."

"No. You're still dazed and you might be struck again."

"But I've got to try something. I've got to see if I'm all right now."

Ames was puzzled. "What are you talking about?"

Ros, too, had been bewildered by his chum's actions, but now a slow smile tugged at his mouth corners.

"Ray, you rascal, you did try it, didn't you?"

"Sure, but I've got to find out if it—"

"What are you two talking about?" demanded Ames. Across the field Doc Halsey was seen approaching, familiar black bag gripped in his hand. Beside him Pete Smith was running while he gave a frenzied explanation of what had happened.

"Maybe it wouldn't hurt to let him try his luck since he's so insistent about batting," said Ros.

"Come on, Al, throw one in," appealed Ray. He had broken away from the hold of his friends and now he stood a trifle weakly at the plate, waving a bat toward the empty mound.

For a moment all the Clarkville players were bewildered. They stood immobile, amazed at the grit displayed by their teammate. He had been struck on the temple by a thrown ball and yet there he was again ready for more.

"Let's go!" shrilled Charlie Minor.

That one cry seemed to break the tension and the players scurried to their positions. Ames strode toward the plate then halted, eyes narrowed and a trifle worried as Ray swayed slightly in the batter's box. In the stands a hush had fallen as eager Clarkville and Glendale students watched the drama being enacted before their eyes.

Everyone sensed that something momentous had occurred. Some grim, powerful urge must be prompting this Clarkville player to go back to the plate after he had been struck by a ball and rendered half unconscious. Yet, only two boys in that entire crowd actually realized the true depth of that drama—the courageous fight against fear being waged by one stout-hearted lad.

Again Ray felt a trifle nervous as he waited for Al Larson to let loose with the pitch. His muscles were tense with the pressure of the moment. Would he be afraid? This was the question that plagued him.

Suddenly he had no further time for thought. The ball was hurtling toward him. His hands were warm and moist on the handle of his bat. His keen eyes watched the flight of the ball. Suddenly they telegraphed a message to his brain and the brain set his muscles into smooth flowing action. He swung easily, sharply. Bert's joyous shout rent the air as the ball swept back over third base for a clean hit.

Again Al Larson poured over a fast ball. It came in high and inside. It was almost a wild pitch. It came arcing straight toward Ray's head. He appeared to wait until the last moment before stepping out of the way. Then came a third fast pitch. Ray stepped into it and the smashing, solid impact of bat on horsehide sent the ball high and deep. Jack Lowell made a half-hearted attempt to chase the ball, then gave up as he watched it bounce on top of the fence and drop over to the field beyond.

Ray threw the bat to the ground and capered around the plate in a dance of joy.

"I did it! It worked! I'm all right. I wasn't afraid."

"Good boy," shouted Bert. "That was a wallop! Do that all the time."

Ray grabbed Bert around the waist and started to jig around the diamond with him.

"There is something the matter with that lad," announced Ames to Ros, who had remained by the bench instead of taking his regular position in the field.

Doc Halsey shook his head. "That rap on the head must have affected him."

"It sure did," said Ros with a laugh, "but not the way you think."

Ames looked puzzled and started toward Ray.

"Ray! Stop that! Here's the doctor to look at that head of yours. Sure you're not faint?"

"Coach, I'm all right," shrilled Ray. His face was aflame with rich pleasure. His eyes glowed. "I did it! I'm not afraid any more."

"What *are* you raving about?"

"It's all over!" said Ray. "I stood up there and the ball came toward me and I wasn't afraid of it."

"Will someone please tell me what's going on?" said Ames.

"I think I can help," said Ros. "Ray's too excited to talk." He paused and flashed Ray a warm, understanding grin. "Ray just tried an experiment with himself as the victim and it worked."

"I still don't understand," protested the Clarkville mentor.

Ray dropped his voice and his face grew serious. "I can tell you now, Coach—now that it's all over. I've been afraid."

"Afraid of what?"

"Afraid of being hit by a ball," replied Ray and his eyes clouded with memory of the agony he had gone through. "Ever since I was struck by a ball in the Springfield game, I've been too scared to even swing at pitches. I trembled and shook, and perspiration would come out all over me because I dreaded being hit again.

"Several days ago Ros and Tom and Bert and the others were talking about baseball and I told them I was worried about losing my place on the team. Ros knew how scared I was at the plate and he said jokingly that what I needed was another rap on the head. When I failed to snap out of it, I thought it was worth a try. So I—"

"You mean you deliberately stepped into Larson's pitch just now?" Ames' eyes were brilliant with shock and surprise.

"That's what I did," responded Ray quietly. "I decided it would make me or break me. I don't know— maybe it's just a superstitious belief and maybe it *does* work, but all I can say is that I'm not afraid any more. I can hit and I'm my old self."

"Now you're talking!" breathed Ros. "We need your hitting."

"It seems almost unbelievable," said Ames.

Ray touched his arm and his eyes were bright with hope and anticipation. Perhaps his glance was a trifle feverish. His head was one dull ache, but he thrust this pain aside. A burning desire to play against Glendale leaped through his veins.

"I'd like to play today, Coach. Do I get the chance?"

The Clarkville coach glanced hopelessly at Doc Halsey.

"I'll want to look at you, Ray," said the medical man. He approached Ray, made him walk back to the bench and sit down. He spent several minutes examining Ray's head with sensitive, probing fingers.

In the meantime Clarkville finished up its practice and the two teams prepared to begin the game.

Ames came over to the bench with the starting line-up in his hand. He gazed soberly at Doc Halsey.

"Well?"

"He seems to be all right. But he ought to go to the Infirmary for a more thorough examination. Might even take an X-ray."

"Please, Coach. Let me play. I've got to make good." There was an urgent appeal in Ray's voice. "Let me try." He turned to the doctor. "Please, Doc, I'll do anything you say, but let me play. I promise to go straight to the Infirmary after the game if you say yes."

Halsey looked troubled. "Any headache, Ray?"

"I did have but it's going away now."

"I don't like to do this but I think you might play a few innings. However, if you begin to feel dizzy or weak, let me know at once."

"Thanks, Doc!" Ray turned to Ames. "Can I play?"

Ames grinned ruefully. "I don't believe anyone would have the right to prevent a boy, who is so anxious to make his team that he'd risk his life to overcome a weakness, from playing. It looks like you've earned the right to play today."

CHAPTER X

ONCE Ray had been given the opportunity to rejoin the squad in an active capacity, he lost no time in proving to the Clarkville coach that the latter's reluctant decision had been a wise one.

In the opening inning of the Glendale game Tom Raynor retired the visitors without anyone reaching first base. But when Clarkville came in to bat, Charlie Minor started the fireworks with a screaming two-bagger into deep center field. Bob Banks advanced Charlie to third with a slow grounder on which the Glendale shortstop could make no other play save at first.

Steve Haley, the Glendale hurler, then became too cautious and in an attempt to keep from feeding Ros any good balls to hit at, finally issued a free trip to first. And that was the picture—Charlie on third, Ros at first and one gone—when Ray stepped in the batter's box.

His head still ached and there was a slight weakness in all his limbs. But despite this handicap, his eyes were bright with anticipation. He had thrown off the shackles of his fear. He was free and he was eager to once again make good in the eyes of his teammates.

Haley tried to nip the outside corner with a sharp-breaking curve but missed. Then came another ball, humming swiftly but low and inside. Not wishing to load the bases with another walk, Haley shot a fast one right down the middle. It had a hop on it but Ray's keen eyes judged it correctly. The bat left his shoulders in a smooth, effortless arc and struck the weaving sphere at the right moment.

Crack! Heads lifted in the stands to watch the swift flight of the ball through the air. Ray's hands tingled from the impact of the hit and he was grinning. There was no need to look where that ball was going. The stinging sensation in his hands, the solid "feel" of a well-hit ball, and the fierce yelling of the crowd told him he had poled another four-master.

"That's the way to hit them!" shouted one leather-lunged baseball addict in the midst of the packed throng in back of the Clarkville bench.

"What a home run!"

"Looks like Ray Hennessey has found the range again!"

Ray was flushed and grinning widely when he crossed the plate and gripped the hands of Charlie and Ros who had scored ahead of him.

"We're off, Ray. Thanks to you," said Charlie.

"That was a swell hit," praised Ros.

"It felt good," admitted Ray. His face turned serious as the three boys started toward the bench. "You don't know how good it is to stand up there and not be afraid."

Ros nodded. "You've certainly got plenty of sand in your system. You took a chance letting yourself get beaned again, just to see if that fool crack I made about another whack on the head fixing you up was the right medicine."

"It was worth it," insisted Ray. "Besides, it worked, didn't it?"

All three lads wheeled sharply around as Jack Lowell stepped into a fast ball and lined it out toward left center. It looked like it might go for extra bases, but at the last moment, the leftfielder, who had fled across the outfield grass like a racing antelope, stuck out his glove and the ball plummeted into it.

"That was plain luck," groaned Charlie.

"Too bad, Jack," said Ros as Jack grumbled and trudged back from first where he had run, thinking the ball was safely hit.

"Just a little more distance on that one," said Ray, "and you would have had a triple."

"Yeah, I know," replied Jack dismally, "but a miss is as good as a mile."

Bert kept the Clarkville rally alive, however, with a hot single over second base and when the centerfielder bobbled the ball momentarily in short center, he hoofed it all the way to second and made it with a daring slide.

"Come on, gang! Let's get another run!" exhorted

Ray. He was jubilant now. All the old spirit had returned to him. He was eager and anxious to be on the move.

Bill Prudy tried hard to comply with the urgent requests of his yelling teammates, but the Glendale flinger bore down and induced him to lift a pop foul to the catcher.

"Better luck next time, Bill," said Ray as he jogged out toward his leftfield patrol spot. "We've got a nice three-run lead and if Tom is in his usual good form we ought to be sitting pretty."

And for the next four innings it appeared that Tom was in excellent fettle. During that time not a Glendale batter reached first. Tom sent three of the visitors back to the bench on strikes, and only one succeeded in lifting a ball out of the infield.

In the meantime, Clarkville had been pecking away at the offerings of Steve Haley. The Light and Dark Blue players were hitting safely in each frame, but except for the opening display, they were unable to put enough of their hits together in one string to produce some runs. As for Ray, when he appeared at the plate in the third inning he was purposely passed.

The fifth inning came up and Tom suddenly found himself in a jam. With a two-and-two count on the first batter, Tom elected to throw a knuckler and the ball got out of control, striking the Glendale player in the ribs.

Hodgson, the shortstop, then sent a high hopper

bounding down to Bill Prudy. The latter had to race to his right and with a desperate lunge, he managed to knock the ball down. Intent on making a double killing, he threw to Pete Smith while he was still out of the position.

Pete leaped high in the air for Bill's wild toss but could not snare it. As a result, each runner advanced a base before Jack could retrieve the sphere and whip it back to the infield.

"Don't let that bother you, Tom!" sang out Ray. "We've got to make the game interesting."

"Careful you don't make it too interesting," responded some caustic voice in the crowd.

Tom braced enough to fling three fast strikes past the Glendale rightfielder, but the next batter crossed him up and caught a curve on the end of his bat, lacing it into short left center. Ray galloped in for the ball, saw the runner on third scoring and without halting his forward motion, rifled the ball to Bert. The latter took the throw on one bounce and tagged the second runner for the out.

A great roar rose from the stands at Ray's splendid throw which had cut off a run at the plate. Of course, the batter went down to second on the play. The value of Ray's action was borne out a moment later when the Glendale catcher, notably a dangerous hitter, walloped a double against the short right field fence to tally the boy from second base.

Tom appeared to be slightly unnerved by the play

and gave a good one to the next batter. The batter
struck savagely at a waist-high pitch and sent it humming along the foul stripe. It was a low liner that just
cleared Bob Bank's head. Somehow Ray raced in and
got his hands on the ball for the second out. He shot
the ball back to second in an attempt to double the
runner there, but the latter had already scurried back
to the bag.

Further danger was averted when Tom forced the
ensuing batsman to bounce a slow roller down to Charlie. Charlie picked it up and raced to the bag to make
the putout unassisted.

In Clarkville's half of the same inning, Jimmy Ames'
charges loaded the bases and then failed to score. Ros
popped to the second baseman but Ray was given a base
on balls. It wasn't a deliberate pass, but Haley was
taking no chances with Ray and preferred to miss the
corners to giving Ray a good ball to strike at.

Jack was also passed and when Bert beat out an infield
hit the Clarkville rooters went into a frenzy, clamoring
for more runs. Unfortunately the weaker half of the
Light and Dark Blue batting line-up was due for serv-
ice. Bill Prudy prolonged the inning with several fouls
and then bounced into a double play to end the suspense.

The sixth inning was uneventful, but in the seventh
Glendale managed to tie it up when Ros and Jack collided in deep right center as both were chasing a line
drive. The ball dropped between them and, though both

lads were only shaken up, the batter stretched the hit into a triple before Ros could relay the ball into the infield. Glendale pushed the tying tally across on a looping Texas leaguer behind first.

Clarkville came to bat in the last half of the seventh, grim and fully determined to regain the lead.

"Let's get that run back," urged Ray as Bob Banks prepared to step to the plate.

"We'll get it," predicted Bert. "The breaks were with them just now."

"Too bad we had to bump into one another," said Ros to Jack. "To tell you the truth I forgot to call out for it."

"So did I," murmured Jack.

Bob Banks was impatient to hit safely and lashed at a bad ball which the Glendale third baseman took on one hop for an easy out. Ros took a swinging strike at a sweeping curve ball, let two low ones go by, then punched a safety over second.

"Come on, Ray! Bring Ros home!"

"Let's have another four-bagger!"

"Make him walk you!"

These were some of the urgent calls which reached Ray from the stands as he took his stance at the plate. He let his glance drift out to the short right field fence. That barrier was ideal for a left-handed batter. It was natural for Ray to hit to that field and it gave him a surge of pleasure to see how the Glendale outfielders backed up toward the fence, playing him very deeply.

Haley's first offering was wide and Ray made no attempt to swing at it. Ray had received instructions from Ames to force Haley to pitch to him and that if Haley insisted on walking him, to take his base on balls without trying to straighten out one of the bad ones for a hit.

The second pitch was equally wide and as the ball left Haley's fingers, Ros dashed for second. However, the Glendale backstop had been expecting such a move. Stepping wide of the plate, he caught the ball and snapped it back on a line to the keystone sacker who tagged Ros a split second before he touched the base with his spikes.

After this play the catcher walked out to the mound and held a little conference. Ray suspected that the Glendale strategy would be changed now. With two out and the bases empty they no doubt would elect to pitch to him.

And Ray was correct. The third pitch was a hard one right down the middle. Ray did not offer at it. He let the fourth go by which was also a called strike. Then, he took a hitch in his trousers, set himself carefully and waited for Haley's delivery.

There was the long wind-up, the flick of an arm, then the horneting flight of a twirling white sphere. It came in fast and hard, shooting wide, then cutting sharply across the outside corner. Ray leaned forward slightly and swung, meeting the ball solidly and sending it high and far into right field.

The ball kept rising after it cleared the infield and Ray was rounding second by the time it soared over the distant right field barrier. It was another smashing home run and it put Clarkville in the lead again.

The Light and Dark Blue nine added another marker on successive doubles by Jack and Bert before a relief hurler was rushed in for duty to stem the tide of Clarkville base hits.

Thus it was 5 to 3 in favor of the home squad at the start of the eighth. Tom appeared to grow stronger as the game progressed and the only hit off his delivery in the last two frames came in the first half of the ninth with two gone. Tom quickly disposed of the next batter and Clarkville's unbeaten record was preserved.

It was a jubilant squad of boys that jogged into the gymnasium after the game. There was talk of an undefeated season and some of the boys ventured the hope that they would make the All-Star team.

"There'll be no stopping us now," affirmed Bert as he prepared to go into a steaming shower. "With Ray knocking over the fences we're a sure bet to be State Scholastic Champions."

"Not so fast," warned Tom, shedding his uniform shirt. "Don't forget Springfield has an unblemished record. They've been winning right along and by more convincing scores than we have chalked up."

"Here's hoping that both teams go undefeated through the season," said Ray. "Then we'll have to play those chaps again."

Ros grinned. "You're aching for another shot at Himber's pitching, aren't you?"

"I sure am."

"Do you blame him?" asked Bert. "Nothing I'd like better myself."

"Well, there's only two more games to go," informed Charlie Minor. "One with Greenwich and the other with Stamford."

"By the way, Ray," said Ros, "I guess you know you're tied with Fred Dressen of Springfield for home run honors in the state."

"No? Am I?"

"Sure. The two you walloped today brings your total up to seven. Dressen has been knocking the old apple around lately. He hit two round-trippers yesterday against Walton, and your friend Himber shut those babies out with four hits."

"The fellow's good," stated Tom.

"You can pitch rings around him any day," countered Bert loyally.

"I'm not so sure."

"You didn't notice him shutting us out, did you?" demanded Ray.

"No, but he may have had an off day."

"Heck," said Bert, "you're only beginning to round into form. You're still a little underweight from your illness. You're stuff was breaking better today than it has all season and there was plenty of hop to your last one."

"Nothing can stop us," said Ray. "We'll take Greenwich and Stamford and then we'll lick Springfield."

"Glad you fellows feel that way," broke in Jimmy Ames as he strolled over to the group with Doc Halsey at his side. "I think you can do it, but it'll mean playing heads-up ball all the way."

Doc Halsey stepped close to Ray and touched his arm. "Go and take your shower, Ray," the medical man directed kindly. "I'm staying here to see that you don't sneak away. I want to examine that head of yours."

"Oh, I feel fine now, Doc," protested Ray.

"I'm glad to hear it," responded Halsey dryly, "but that still doesn't change matters. You are going to spend a day or two in the Infirmary. We can't take any chances. You may have suffered some injury that will only make itself felt later."

Ray continued to protest but to no avail. Doc Halsey was adamant, and when Ames and even his chums advised him to comply with the medical man's suggestion, Ray acquiesced.

It developed, however, that the doctor's fears were unfounded. X-rays revealed no injury or fracture and after a day of rest in the Infirmary, Ray was released.

Three days later Clarkville met and defeated Greenwich. Tom pitched air-tight ball all the way, letting Greenwich down with four singles and fanning ten.

The final score was 7 to 0 and Ray sparked the assault with two home runs and a double.

The Light and Dark Blue nine seemed to pick up momentum as the season wore on. All the players were filled with the winning spirit. They played alertly, making very few mistakes and capitalizing on every scoring opportunity. The defense improved and everyone began to hit. They overwhelmed Stamford 14 to 5. Tom hurled the first three innings and yielded two singles, during which time the Light and Dark Blue squad handed him a 6 to 0 lead. After that, Ames took him out to rest him for the all-important game with Springfield, since the latter team, by beating Bridgeport and St. Luke's also remained undefeated.

Ray hit two successive home runs in the first and second innings and later in the game Bert and Jack chipped in with round-trip blows. Ray finished the day with a double and a single in five official appearances at the plate. The only time Stamford could get him out was when the centerfielder raced all the way to the fence to pull down Ray's terrific line drive in the eighth inning.

CHAPTER XI

HIMBER'S TREACHERY

DURING the entire week following Clarkville's smashing victory over Stamford, all the local newspapers were filled with accounts of the impending diamond battle between Clarkville and Springfield.

Since the first game had been played at Alumni Field, it was decided to shift this game to the Springfield diamond. The move, while made in all fairness, figured to favor Springfield because the latter school's diamond had a deep right field which would tend to reduce Ray's chances of clearing the fence with home runs. Ray, being left-handed, was inclined to pull his blows toward right field. There was every reason to suspect, therefore, that the outfielders might gather in his long drives.

On the other hand the left field fence was closer to the plate. This factor would favor Dressen who was a right-handed batter.

Needless to say, all the Clarkville students were excited by the prospect of the impending crucial game. Teachers had considerable difficulty making the boys pay attention to the lectures because there was a constant undercurrent of excited talk in all the classrooms.

The day of the big game finally arrived and the conversation was even more animated among the players themselves, as the special bus transporting the Clarkville team to Springfield rolled along the smoothly paved state highway.

"It won't be long now," said Tom with a grin as he turned in his seat to face Ray and Ros.

"How does your arm feel?" inquired Ray.

"Never better," stated Tom.

"Think you can stand those Springfield chaps on their heads?"

"Can't guarantee it, but I'll certainly try." Tom flashed Ray a friendly smile. "But what about our home run ace? Is he going to wrap a couple of four-baggers around Mr. Himber's ears this afternoon?"

Ray's face turned grim. His bronzed cheeks were hard and smooth. "I'll be swinging from my heels every time I'm up there."

"You just hit one home run and you're sure to make the All-Star team," Ros assured him.

"Well," said Ray seriously, "I sure would like to win a place on that team, but right now I'm more interested in having Clarkville whip Springfield."

Bert slapped him on the back. "That's true team spirit and it's the kind of spirit that will lick Springfield!"

When the special bus rolled into the extensive grounds of Springfield Academy, the Light and Dark

Blue players were surprised to see that the welcoming delegation was composed of the entire home nine. This was an unusually nice gesture and it pleased Ames immensely.

"Springfield is proving that it has real sports," said Ames.

"Oh-oh," observed Bert and nudged Ray. "There's our two friends—Himber and Dressen."

There was no opportunity for Ray to answer his chum for the bus had rolled to a stop and the boys were beginning to pile out. Ray and his friends soon noted that various Springfield players were pairing off to chaperone the Clarkville lads to the gymnasium where they could change into their uniforms.

"Hi, fellows!"

Ray and Bert gave a start of shock and surprise as Himber and Dressen detached themselves from the welcoming committee and came over to greet them.

"Hello," grunted Ray and Bert together.

Instinctively they shook hands with the two Springfield lads who appeared to be very friendly.

"Welcome to Springfield and may the best team win," murmured Himber, his mouth twisted in a smile. Ray noted, however, a strange malicious gleam in the depths of Himber's eyes and he was vaguely uneasy.

"What's happened to you chaps?" queried Bert, also suspicious.

"Nothing," responded Dressen blandly. "We just want to make you feel at home. Every Springfield player was assigned to some Clarkville player to see that he was given every attention."

"Well, that—that is nice," grunted Bert.

"Come along," said Himber a trifle brusquely. "We'll show you to the gym."

Ray and Bert exchanged puzzled glances but fell into step beside the two Springfield ball players. Ahead of them other boys were walking rapidly toward the great ivy-clad building that housed Springfield's gymnasium, basketball court, locker rooms and swimming pool.

The baseball diamond was set almost beside the gymnasium and already the various candy and soft drink vendors were plying their wares. As they approached one portable wagon laden with candy, popcorn, soft drinks and brick ice cream, Himber led them aside.

"Let's have something to drink. What do you say?"

"No, thanks," said Ray. "Not before a game. Besides that soda has too much gas in it."

"Not soda," protested Himber. "A little orangeade would pep us all up."

"I'm game," said Bert quickly.

Ray grinned. "Never saw you refuse to eat or drink anything."

"That's settled, then," said Himber. He gestured to the wizened old man who was tending the wagon. "Four glasses of orangeade."

The man nodded and hurried to fill the order, passing out paper cups filled to the brim with clear, cold orangeade. There was a sudden loud roar overhead and Himber shouted.

"Look at that big plane, will you?"

Ray and Bert set down their drinks to lift their eyes to the blue vault of the sky. A huge silver-winged plane was droning past overhead, traveling at a great rate of speed.

"Must be one of those Flying Fortresses," observed Ray.

"Wouldn't be surprised," grunted Dressen.

At last the huge plane sped out of sight and the boys turned their attention back to their drinks. Ray picked up his cup, lifted it to his lips and sipped the drink slowly. Over the lip of the cup his eyes met those of Himber and found them strangely intense and not at all friendly.

Beside Ray, Bert gulped his drink down.

"That hit the spot," said the stout lad. "I really was thirsty."

Himber gave him a mocking stare and his lips twisted in a leering grin.

"Glad you liked it."

A group of Springfield students raced by, yelling and shouting, intent on getting good seats for the ball game though they were even too early for practice. Ray turned to watch them. Then, in swinging back to his drink, his arm struck the cup and sent it toppling to the ground.

The cup was crushed and its contents trickled out on the ground.

"Gosh!" moaned Ray. "That was clumsy of me."

Himber snorted and his face was unpleasant. "I'll treat you to another."

"No thanks. I've had enough." Ray's eyes shifted from Himber to the ground at his feet. "Say, look at that!" He gestured with his hand toward a gray kitten which was lapping up the tiny pool of orangeade. "That kitten must be thirsty."

"Darned if that kitten doesn't look as if it were drunk," added Bert.

"Sure enough," agreed Ray, perplexed. He watched the kitten pad away from the spot of moisture. It swayed from side to side, then suddenly it halted and curled up in a furry ball near the soda vendor's wagon. In a moment it was asleep.

Bert stifled a yawn with the back of his hand. "Darned if that kitten didn't go right off to sleep."

Ray's glance lifted, speculative and cold. Bert yawned again. His eyes looked sleepy. Ray peered down at the contented shape of the kitten, then swung to confront the malicious grin which was warping the mouth of Bart Himber.

"Gosh, I feel sort of sleepy myself," moaned Bert.

"Sure you do!" Ray's voice cracked like a whip. It startled the stout lad into temporary awareness.

"What's the matter?"

"Plenty!" Ray rasped. The bitter hostility in his eyes created taut lines around his mouth. Anger quickened his words when he spoke to Himber. "Of all the dirty tricks to play, Himber! You put something in that orangeade. That's why you were so anxious to have us look at that airplane and that's why that kitten fell right off to sleep after lapping up my spilled drink!"

"You're crazy," retorted Himber blandly, but behind the Springfield pitcher, Fred Dressen couldn't keep the wicked triumph from his face.

Bert tried to stifle a yawn. "No wonder that drink tasted kind of bitter."

"I noticed it, too," murmured Ray, "but I thought I was imagining it." Knotted muscles stiffened along the hard line of his jaw. "So that's your sneaking way of getting revenge after being licked in a straight fight! You deliberately doctored those drinks!"

Himber laughed suddenly. It was a surly, confident gesture. "You'll never be able to prove it."

"I'm not going to try," replied Ray harshly.

"Gosh, Ray, you're right," Bert groaned. "I can hardly keep my eyes open. They did that to keep us out of the game."

Ray clenched his fists and a savage glint crept into his eyes.

"Luckily I didn't drink much," he said. Then he turned to the other boys. "You may keep one of us out of the game but as sure as shooting, I'm going to see that neither of you sneaks play today, if I have to take you on together."

With that angry threat Ray strode forward. His eyes were narrow slits in his anger-reddened face, and he was ready to fight both these boys in answer to their treacherous trick.

"Put up your hands, Himber. You're first."

Himber grinned mirthlessly and said, "Sure. This is a pleasure."

Ray started to swing a left when Jimmy Ames' strident voice issuing from the entrance to Springfield's gymnasium, reached him.

"Ray! Bert! Come along. Get into your suits!"

"All right, Coach. We'll be right there," said Ray. His smoldering gaze hit Himber and Dressen with a withering and compelling intensity. "I'll be seeing you fellows again and the sooner the better!"

With that grim warning Ray led Bert away from the two smirking Springfield boys. Bert could hardly stand on his feet, as the overpowering urge for sleep deadened his muscles.

"If I could only get my hands on those fellows," gritted Bert, close to tears—so great was his anger. "I can't stay awake. I'll miss the game and I've been looking forward to it."

"Never mind, Bert," rapped Ray. "We'll beat Springfield and after that I'm going to look up those two fellows."

As soon as they entered the Clarkville dressing quarters, Ray's teammates noticed Bert yawning. Bert sat down on a bench. Slowly he sagged on his side, his head pillowed on the hard wood. Instantly he was asleep.

"What's the matter with Bert?" demanded Ros, concern putting ragged lines in his cheeks.

"Good night! Look at him!" grunted Charlie Minor. "Bert's sound asleep."

"What is it?" repeated Ros.

Ray was harsh with his answer. "A couple of sneaks pulled a mean trick on us, slipped some sleeping powders in orangeade while we weren't looking—after inviting us to the treat."

"Who was it?"

"Never mind."

"You mean Bert'll sleep right through the game?" demanded Charlie.

"Just that," snapped Ray tersely. "Bert gulped down an entire cup of orangeade and got the full dose of the powders." Ros and Charlie drew close while Ray quickly gave them an account of what had transpired.

"I might have known it was those chaps," said Ros. "It's just like them. We'll get even. Of all the low tricks—"

Conversation broke off at the sudden approach of Jimmy Ames. He uttered a startled gasp when he saw Bert's sleeping form.

"What's happened to Bert?"

Ray told him but without revealing the names of Himber or Dressen.

"Why, it's unbelievable!" exclaimed the Clarkville mentor. "Who was responsible?"

Ray glanced apologetically at Ames. "If it's all the same to you, Coach, I'd rather not say."

"But this is a matter calling for disciplinary action. I intend to take it up with Clyde Mallory, the Springfield coach. You must tell me."

"Don't you see that I couldn't tell you?" Ray's voice held a pleading note. "I know who they are and I'd like to handle this."

"But Bert cannot play and you may be forced out of the game yourself."

"I only had a little of the orangeade since I spilled most of mine." In spite of his effort to conceal it, Ray was forced to yawn. He was feeling a trifle drowsy himself. "Please don't ask me to tell you who it was, Coach."

Ames looked displeased. "All right. I'll have to use Cal Wilson in Bert's place. This is one game I wanted Clarkville to win and to do it we'll need every regular playing in top form. With Bert out and you half-drowsy yourself, we'll be handicapped."

Ray's chin lifted defiantly. "We'll win this game. I for one will play my heart out to help Clarkville."

"And we're with you!" chorused a host of loyal voices.

CHAPTER XII

AN UNDEFEATED SEASON

A LUSTY shout rose from the closely-packed stands surrounding the playing field at Springfield as Bart Himber whipped a fast strike past Charlie Minor to start the long-awaited crucial diamond contest. And when Himber proceeded to fan Charlie on two more pitches the students went into a frenzy of delight.

Himber had little trouble in disposing of Bob Banks and Ros, and in a twinkling Clarkville found itself out on the field. But Tom was in fine shape and got by the first frame without experiencing any difficulty.

Ray was feeling drowsy and his muscles felt lax and loose when he strode to the plate. He set himself grimly, striving to fight off the effects of the sleeping potion while Himber, poised gracefully on the mound, sneered at him in open contempt.

"Here's where I put you to sleep, Hennessey!" taunted Himber.

"Play ball and shut up," replied Ray harshly. "You and I will talk later."

Grim and determined as Ray was, some of the energy had been drained from him and his timing was poor.

He missed a wide curve, and then misjudged Himber's tantalizing knuckler and popped to the first baseman.

Three innings rolled by and Himber continued to mow down every Clarkville batter to face him. He was fast. His control was excellent and he was pitching to "spots." But Tom matched him pitch for pitch, putting every fibre of his being into each throw. And so the top half of the fourth inning arrived with neither team having been able to get a man on base.

Once again Clarkville proved impotent at the plate and Springfield came to bat with the home rooters clamoring for some hits and runs.

"Come on, gang! Let's beat that Clarkville bunch!"

"Get a hit, Flack!" called another to the lead-off batter.

Out in left field, Ray kept moving around, fighting off the lethargy in his muscles, the heaviness that weighted down his eyelids.

"Mow them down, Tom!" he shouted. "Get them out, one-two-three!"

Tom worked hard on Flack, pitching carefully, but Flack picked out a toss to his liking, and pounded it over second for the first hit of the game. Tom turned on the heat and whiffed the next batter on four straight pitches. Then, his control ebbed and he lost Ryerson, the third baseman, and gave him a walk.

Ray's face clouded as Fred Dressen swaggered to the plate. Tom had retired Dressen on an infield grounder in the second inning, but could Tom fool him again? Ray was worried. Tom bore down and got two strikes on the Springfield backstop, then tossed two balls. Dressen fouled one off and let another wide one go by to bring the count to three-and-two.

Crack! It was a dreaded sound to Ray. Dressen had swung savagely on Tom's next offering. The ball rose over the infield, arcing toward deep left center. The boys on the base paths were running swiftly.

Ray dug in his spikes and churned toward the distant fence. He saw with a surge of dismay that the sphere would sweep past him. It struck the fence on the fly. Ray played it cleverly on the rebound as he saw Dressen rounding second.

Anger rippling through him, Ray cocked his arm and catapulted the ball toward Bob Banks. It would be a close play and Ray gritted his teeth praying desperately that his throw would be accurate enough to cut down Dressen. A great cloud of dust rose around the hot corner, and Ray and the crowd waited tensely while the umpire squatted down, peering through the thick gray cloud. Then Ray's heart leaped with joy when he saw the base arbiter jerk his thumb over his shoulder. Dressen had been tagged out!

Ray felt better. There were two out, though a pair of runs had trickled across the plate. Tom braced and forced the next batter to line out to Bill Prudy at short.

"Let's have some action at the plate!" pleaded Ames when the Light and Dark Blue nine charged in from the diamond. "You, Ray! Are you all right?"

"A little light-headed but I'll be all right," said Ray.

"Have to keep you in there," said Ames. "Get on base!"

Ray nodded grimly, selected his favorite bat from the row in front of the Clarkville bench and prepared to face the arrogant, confident figure of Bart Himber.

"You're wasting your time, Hennessey!" said Dressen, squatting behind the plate, his eyes mocking the Clarkville lad.

Ray gave him a cold, hard glance but said nothing. Inwardly he was seething with rage, but he forced his cheeks to remain smooth and immobile. He missed the first pitch and his lips tightened when the crowd roared in glee. Again they roared when he misjudged Himber's floater and dribbled a foul to the right of first base.

"You're pressing!" he cautioned himself. "Take it easy. Don't let those chaps rile you. That's what they want."

Himber wasted one, tempting Ray with a sweeping curve but the latter let it go by for a ball. Suddenly Ray felt the tension leave his muscles. Some of the sleepiness was wearing off. He felt loose and supple and strangely confident. When the next pitch came hurtling toward the plate, he met it swiftly, his wrists snapping at the moment of impact, adding impetus to the ball's lofty flight.

Out on the pitching mound Bart Himber tossed his glove to the ground in a gesture of fury and disgust.

In the crowded stands Clarkville and Springfield rooters alike roared in glee as the ball sped beyond the reach of the sprinting outfielders, to clear the fence in right-center field.

Jack and Ros greeted Ray when he had completed his victorious jaunt around the base paths.

"That's all we needed!" exclaimed Ros. "We're off!"

"What a hit!"

"I think I'll take a sleeping powder if that's the way it affects a person," said Ros with a grin.

Himber was so unnerved by Ray's round-trip blow that he walked Jack, and was touched for a single by Cal Wilson, catching in place of Bert. Himber bore down savagely, attempting to burn the ball past the Light and Dark Blue swingers. He got Bill Prudy and Pete Smith on infield flies, but Tom tied the score with a clean single into center field which tallied Jack. But that was all, Charlie Minor, again striking out to end the inning.

The fifth inning sped by with neither team threatening. Then, in the sixth Ray led off again and drew a base on balls, after fouling off a number of Himber's pitches. Jack came through with a single into right field on which Ray was held to one base by a stunning throw from the Springfield rightfielder.

Bill Prudy and Pete Smith again proved easy pickings for the home team hurler, but Tom Raynor lashed a torrid grounder to the right of the shortstop. Ray

was off like an antelope at the crack of the bat and
had rounded third as the fielder knocked the ball down
with his glove.

He saw and heard Dressen yelling for the ball and
setting himself in the base path. Charging down the
chalked line, Ray flung his body in a hook slide, spiked
foot aiming for the plate. He heard the impact of the
ball in Dressen's glove, felt the latter plant the ball
into his side as he slid across the plate. Dimly he heard
the yell of triumph from the Clarkville bench, signify-
ing that the umpire had called him safe, then hot pain
shot through his leg as steel spikes dug into his right
ankle.

Through the dust haze he saw the wicked gleam in
Dressen's eyes and he rose with a cry of rage and pain.
He took a stumbling step toward Dressen and pumped
a right into the latter's face before stumbling and falling.

The umpires rushed up and players from both teams
crowded about the two boys.

"No fighting!" thundered one of the umpires. "Take
it easy, both of you or you'll be chucked out of the
game."

Ray paid no heed to the arbiter. His gaze plucked
at Dressen with a glittering intensity. "You deliberately spiked me!"

"It was an accident," said Dressen, his face reddening as he met the enraged stares of the Clarkville
players.

"Your ankle is bleeding!" announced Ros.

"We'll have to take a look at that," Ames directed.

"Don't take me out," pleaded Ray as he was led away from Dressen.

"That remains to be seen."

Quickly the sock was pulled from Ray's foot, and the coach frowned as he noted the ugly gash in the white flesh. Ray shut his eyes at the pain.

"That's a bad cut," stated Ames.

"Just bandage it up. I can play."

"You won't be able to stand on that ankle."

"I'll stand on it somehow," gritted Ray.

Ames frowned but set about washing out the wound with clean cloths and dabbing it liberally with iodine. Ray winced with pain and sweat studded his brow as the iodine hit the raw cut. Then the gash was bandaged securely and bound with adhesive tape. Someone provided a clean sock and Ray replaced his spiked shoe.

While this was attended to, Himber retired Charlie Minor on a long fly to the outfield.

"How does it feel?" Ames asked, a worried frown creasing his brow.

"All right," said Ray blandly, though it pained him greatly.

"Let's see you walk," insisted Ames.

Ray took a few steps and fresh agony wracked his frame as he strove to walk naturally without limping. Somehow he did it and Ames grudgingly permitted Ray to continue in the game.

Clarkville was in the lead by the slim margin of one run as Springfield came to bat in the last half of the sixth. Unfortunately that lead did not last in this bitter, see-saw struggle. Ryerson doubled along the right field foul line and then Dressen electrified the crowd with a powerful home run over the left field barrier to put Springfield back in the lead, 4 to 3.

Both pitchers were hurling admirable ball but there was no denying the batting prowess of such boys as Ray and his rival, Fred Dressen. As a result of Dressen's tremendous clout, the Light and Dark Blue nine was confronted with the task of again trying to manufacture two runs as had been done in the fourth frame.

Bob Banks was the victim of a strikeout, but Ros lifted the hopes of Ames' charges when he pounded out a single.

"Here comes the cry baby!" taunted Dressen as Ray moved to the plate.

Ray gave him a withering glance. "You coward. I'll pay you back for spiking me, and I'll pay back your sneaking friend for doping up that orangeade."

"How do you aim to do it?" queried Dressen blandly.

"You'll see. But first I'm going to plant one over the right field fence."

"You were just lucky the last time."

Ray's glance turned dim and wild. He gripped his bat tightly and brought it around on the first pitch. It was a solidly hit ball. The throw was a high hard one, rocketing toward the plate with all of Himber's speed behind it, and it swept back toward the outfield with all of the might in Ray's arms and shoulders propelling it.

Once again the partisan rooters were forced to cheer as the ball sailed far over the distant right field fence for Ray's second home run of the day. True, Ray was playing for the rival team, but where is there a baseball fan who can keep from applauding a home run, no matter who the batter?

The entire Clarkville team bunched around Ray to congratulate him after he had made his leisurely circuit of the bases.

"Great hitting!" cheered Ros.

"You're Clarkville's home run king," said Charlie.

"You mean the state home run king," corrected Tom, giving Ray a sound whack on the shoulders. "Dressen will never catch up to Ray now."

Ames approached the group and his pleasure was very evident.

"That was a well-hit ball, Ray. My compliments to you." He turned his attention to the others. "Now let me see you fellows hold that lead. Tom, keep those Springfield fellows from getting on base."

"We'll do our best!" they promised.

Jack and Cal tried to keep the Light and Dark Blue rally going, but Himber showed his mettle by forcing both lads to lift pop flies to the shortstop. Then, in the last half of the seventh Dame Fortune abandoned Clarkville.

Hendricks, the first batter, drove a hot grounder straight at Tom. The latter made a desperate attempt to put his glove down and field the ball but it caromed off his right shin. Tom was knocked to the ground. He stumbled to his feet, staggered after the ball, then fell flat on his face. By the time Charlie had raced into short right field for the ball Hendricks was perched on second.

Immediately the Clarkville infield made an anxious circle about Tom. He was helped to his feet but the pain was intense.

"That was a nasty wallop," said Bill Prudy.

"Can you stand on it?" asked Ames, worried lines bracketing the corners of his mouth.

"I'll try." While they watched he limped around on the mound. "Let me have the ball."

Time was called in again by the umpires and Tom took a short wind-up. Then as he tried to put his weight on his right foot, he lost his balance and the ball got away from him. It sailed over Cal Wilson's glove for a wild pitch and Hendricks dashed to third.

Ames rushed out again. "What's the matter?"

"I'm sorry, Coach. I can't put any weight on the foot."

Ames' face turned grim. "Too bad. We need you in there, but it's obvious you can't go on. Better get over to the gym and have the Springfield doctor have a look at your leg. I'll have to put in Dale Weston to pitch in your place."

Although Tom hated to leave the game, and the entire team dreaded the results if any other pitcher faced the Springfield powerhouse, there was nothing else to be done under the circumstances. Accordingly, young Dale Weston, a promising southpaw, was rushed into the box.

Weston warmed up for quite some time but when time was called and his first offering was pasted into center field for a clean single, Ames began to wonder if his choice of a relief hurler had been a wise one. His selection had been largely influenced by the fact that most of Springfield's batters were right handers and, therefore, a southpaw pitcher would be more apt to hold them down.

One run was in as a result of that single and the score was again tied 5–5. Weston induced the next batter to force the runner at first going into second, but Bart Himber drove a long double past Ros in center and this hit was followed by another single and two more markers were in, putting Springfield ahead 7 to 5.

Ray made a sparkling catch of a line drive over near the foul line for the second out, and then Weston fanned Seward, the left fielder for the final out of the inning.

It was a grim, determined aggregation of players that came in for the first half of the eighth inning, but Himber wove a spell around the bats of Bill, Pete and

Tom, and chalked up a goose egg on the scoreboard for the Light and Dark Blue nine.

Weston got into a jam in the last half of the inning when Dressen doubled with one gone, but Ray came to the rescue with a one-handed stop of a low line drive that appeared to be ticketed for a safety, and doubled Dressen off second with a fine toss to Pete Smith.

Then in the ninth Himber showed signs of tiring. Charlie worked him for a base on balls and Bob followed with a hot single over second, sending Charlie to third. Himber set his jaw grimly, and his eyes were like flaming sparks when he worked on Ros. The Clarkville centerfielder punched a high hopper back toward the shortstop. The latter had to go to his right but he made the catch. Faking a throw to home, he kept Charlie rooted to third, then whipped the ball to first. However, his throw pulled the initial sacker off the bag and all hands were safe.

The crowd roared in eager anticipation as Ray strode to the plate. The bases loaded, Clarkville behind by the margin of two runs! What a setting. For the first time in many days Ray experienced nervousness as he prepared to face an opposing pitcher.

If he could only connect for a hit now. There were none out and this would be Clarkville's last chance to tie up the ball game, especially since Springfield had another time of bat.

Neither Himber nor Dressen said anything to Ray

this time. They were all tense, completely intent on retiring Ray. Would they purposely walk him and force in a run in order to prevent Ray from hitting a home run? Ray thought not, for then the bases would still be loaded with none out.

Himber's first offering was a called strike. The second was a ball and so was the third. Ray swung at the fourth and fouled it over the stands. Himber tried a floater and Ray swung, but again it was a foul. Then Himber missed the inside corner for a ball and there was a full count.

What would Himber throw now? This was the question humming through Ray's mind. He had to outguess the Springfield hurler. In came the pitch. Ray swung. High and far sailed the ball with Ray racing toward first. Then the first base umpire gestured that the ball had cleared the fence but was foul by inches!

Ray groaned and returned to the plate. He saw Himber's snarling, determined face, the arc of the hurler's arm, then the fiery streak of the ball rocketing toward him. Again Ray swung and this time the ball went straight and true. The rightfielder streaked toward the wooden barrier, half climbed the fence in a frantic attempt to spear the ball, but it sailed over his outstretched glove.

Pandemonium broke loose over the diamond. The Clarkville players leaped up from the bench, tossing their hats into the air, shouting in glee as Charlie,

Bob and Ros preceded Ray in the victorious tour around the bases.

It didn't matter that Himber retired the next three men in order. It didn't matter that Springfield still had to come to bat for its half of the ninth. Nothing mattered save that Ray had poled his third home run of the afternoon and had again boosted Clarkville into the lead in this bitter diamond struggle. The score was 9 to 7 in favor of the Light and Dark Blue.

There was no stopping Clarkville after that. Springfield filled the sacks with one out but sensational fielding by Ray in the outfield and Bill Prudy at short pulled Weston out of the hole without a run being scored.

As soon as the final out was made the Clarkville players rushed upon Ray and carried him to their shoulders.

"Hurrah for the State Champions!"

"Hurrah for the home run king!" added Ros.

And thus in laughing triumph the Clarkville nine trooped merrily to their dressing quarters, and all thoughts Ray might have had about Himber and Dressen were forgotten in the universal revelry.

CHAPTER XIII

GOOD NEWS

EVERY boy in the crowded room jointly occupied by
Tom, Bert and Ray in Corbin Hall looked up expectantly as the door swung open and Charlie Minor walked
in. There were a dozen boys in the room, most of them
players on the Clarkville nine, and all of them fondly
hoping that they would be lucky enough to be selected
for the All-Star team.

"Any news yet?" queried Ray, his voice vibrant with
emotion.

"Not a thing," grunted Charlie and managed to
wedge himself on one of the beds between Ray and Ros.

"This suspense is killing me," said Ros.

"And me," added Bert.

"Oh, go on back to sleep," said Ros with a laugh.
"Any fellow that sleeps through the most important
game of the season ought to hang his head in shame."
Ros was referring to the effects of the sleeping potion
Bart Himber had put in Bert's orangeade.

The stocky Light and Dark Blue backstop had been
the butt of many jokes in the few hours that had
elapsed since that game. Though all knew it had been

a mean trick or prank, still they delighted in trying to sting Bert to anger. But this time Bert only grinned and refused to let Ros get the better of him.

Bob Banks broke the short silence which had ensued after Ros' remark to Bert.

"Ames told us the judges would have their decisions in by the evening following our game with Springfield and that notices would be posted in all the residence halls."

"What are you worried about?" grunted Pete Smith. "You won't make the team anyway."

"Maybe not," admitted Bob, "but Ray and Tom and Ros and Bert certainly have a swell chance."

"Don't even talk about it," advised Ray. "The more I think about it the less chance I think I have."

A chorus of dissenting voices broke in upon him.

"Are you crazy?" protested Bert. "You were the leading hitter in our league this season. You hit the most home runs and drove in the most runs and your fielding average was excellent."

"They can't help picking you," added Tom.

"Thanks, fellows," said Ray, reddening. "Hope you're right." He turned to Tom and his cheeks grew serious. "How is your leg?"

Tom felt of his injured shin bone. "Doc Halsey says it's just a severe bone bruise. No fracture. If I'm lucky enough to make the All-Stars he says the leg will be all right for me to pitch in Havana."

"That is good news!" shouted Ray and Bert together, their voices warm with affection for their room-mate.

"And here's more news!" said a new voice as the door swung open again.

"Coach!" the boys said in unison.

Jimmy Ames stepped into the room and his face was ruddy with pleasure. In his hand he held a sheet of paper.

"About the All-Stars?" whispered Ray.

"Yes! The team has been selected and I'm proud to say that Clarkville has placed three players on the squad which will sail for Cuba next week."

"Who are they?" demanded Charlie.

Ames grinned, thoroughly enjoying this moment.

"I figured all you boys would be in this room waiting for the news to break. That's why I came to deliver it in person."

"Don't keep us in suspense," pleaded Ros. "Tell us now."

Ames held up his hands and laughed heartily.

"All right, boys! I guess I've teased you long enough. The lucky lads from Clarkville are Ray Hennessey, Tom Raynor and Ros Hackney!"

"Hurrah!" shouted the boys in the closely packed room.

Charlie and Bob and Pete got up from their seats and rushed around the three fortunate lads and congratulated them.

"Good boy, Ray," said Charlie. "You deserved it."

"Nice going, Tom," said Bob to Ros.

Both Ray and Ros blushed with the praise that was heaped upon them, while Tom, also, was embarrassed by the enthusiastic plaudits of his chums.

"I'd like to personally congratulate all three of you boys," said Ames.

He approached Ray and Tom and Ros and shook hands with them. There was something warm and heartening about that gesture. In it was all of the Clarkville coach's esteem, mingled with a justifiable pride that three of the lads under his tutelage had been judged worthy of representing America against a picked nine of Cuban boys.

"Thanks, Coach," breathed Ray, elation coloring his cheeks with rich red blood. "I guess we all owe it to your coaching."

"Not at all," contradicted Ames. "Of course, I did help, but in the last analysis it was you yourselves who turned the trick. After all, once you were out on the diamond you were on your own and each game was yours to win or lose. I am happy that Clarkville will have three players on the squad and I know Dr. Holbrook, the head master, will join me in these sentiments. As for the rest of you who played such fine ball for Clarkville, I can only say I am sorry that there was not room enough for all of you to win positions with the All-Stars."

"I guess Clarkville won the most places on the team," said Bert.

Ames shook his head.

"No. Our strongest rival, Springfield, also won three places."

"Who are the fellows?" queried Ray tensely.

Ames gave Ray a searching look then said: "Jim Cresset won the second base spot, Fred Dressen took catching honors and Bart Himber will share pitching honors with Tom since it was decided that the All-Stars should have two pitchers."

Ray looked troubled. He asked: "Who were the rest?"

"Bill Scully of St. Luke's will play third," replied Ames, consulting the sheet of paper in his hand. "Al Torrance of Bridgeport will play shortstop, Frank Duane of Glendale, will be at first, and Ed Hinkle of Norwood will be the right fielder."

Soon a fiery discussion was waging back and forth across the room. The boys talked over the merits of various players and mentioned boys they thought should have won places on the team. For a time Ames joined in the conversation, then he took his departure, instructing Ray, Tom and Ros to pay a visit to Dr. Holbrook the following afternoon in reference to a leave of absence from Clarkville, as well as to make arrangements for making up class work that would be missed while they were away on the cruise.

CHAPTER XIV

OFF TO CUBA

"So LONG, America!" shouted Ray with a wave of his arm.

"Hello, Cuba! Here we come!" added Tom.

"The invasion of the tropics is under way," said Ros.

The three boys, together with other members of the Scholastic All-Star baseball squad, were grouped along the rail of the *S. S. Triton* as it steamed out of New York harbor.

It was an exciting moment—a moment which had been eagerly awaited by every lad on the team. It was the Saturday after the fateful Clarkville-Springfield game and with good weather and calm seas they were scheduled to arrive in Havana early Tuesday morning.

Slowly the towering skyscrapers—the famed shore-line of the greatest city in the world—began to recede from view while the cruise ship headed toward the open sea.

It had been one hectic week for Ray and his chums, as well as for the other boys on the All-Star team. They had all met in New York the preceding day and under the direction of Jimmy Ames of Clarkville and

139

Clyde Mallory of Springfield, who had been selected as joint coaches and chaperones of the All-Stars during the cruise, the eager throng of boys had made a short tour of the city.

In special cars hired for the occasion they had visited the Aquarium, General Grant's tomb, driven through the new New York-Queens midtown vehicular tunnel, then later crossed back into the city by way of the famous Tri-Boro Bridge. They had ridden up Fifth Avenue on the double-decker buses, after dismissing the special cars, and had visited the tower of the Empire State building one hundred and two stories above the street.

In the evening the entire group had journeyed to Radio City to see one of the latest motion pictures just released by Hollywood and by the time they returned to their hotel, they all agreed that they were more tired than they would have been if they had played three baseball games.

Early Saturday morning they had visited Yankee Stadium and, with the New York Yankees out of town on a scheduled jaunt through the west, the squad had enjoyed a short workout on the diamond that had seen so many famous baseball games, as well as World Series games.

But now that they were actually on the water and bound for Havana, the boys had a chance to take stock of themselves and rest up a trifle. At least, this was the advice given by the two coaches. However, it soon became obvious that boys in their teens have too much natural energy to be expected to sit still while there are places to be explored on board ship and things to be done.

As for Ray's relations with Bart Himber and Fred Dressen, they had spoken together whenever circumstances demanded it. Otherwise, they avoided each other, though the boys from other schools mingled freely with either group.

Ray finally took his eyes off the rolling sea and spoke to his two chums.

"Let's explore the ship. What do you say?"

"I say it's a good idea!" responded Ros quickly.

"Count me in," added Tom. "This ship is like a floating palace. It must be more than a block long."

"Sure it is," said Ray. "Why you can have a real good hike just walking around the deck a few times."

However, it soon appeared that Jimmy Ames had anticipated this desire on the part of his charges, and had arranged with Captain Morton Blaine to have one of the stewards personally conduct them around the ship.

The party was gathered together quickly and Ames introduced the boys to John Lacey, the steward, a tall, somber-eyed young man who greatly resembled Bart Himber.

"Boys," said Ames, "I want you all to meet John Lacey. He will take us around the boat and show us all the points of interest."

"Hello!" sang out the crowd.

"Glad to meet all of you," acknowledged Lacey. "If you'll follow me, we'll start our tour right now."

They proceeded to a narrow stairway which led to the boat deck, part of which had been set aside as a sport deck. As they were going up the stairs, Ray turned to Ros and said:

"Did you notice how much the steward looks like Himber?"

Ros nodded. "I did. You could almost take them for brothers."

"It's certainly a coincidence," agreed Tom, who had also heard Ray's remark.

"I guess Lacey sees plenty of sights, being stationed on a ship like this. This boat cruises to the West Indies and even makes trips down along the east and west coast of South America." Ros shrugged his shoulders as if he envied Lacey.

On the boat deck they found the lifeboats, fully equipped and ready for launching. Then there was a large space set aside for playing deck tennis, shuffleboard and quoits. Below, was the beautiful promenade deck which circled the entire ship. And in the bow of the ship on the promenade deck was the new tiled outdoor swimming pool.

Then they visited A, B, and C decks, toured the many beautiful lounges, the card room and writing room, the cabaret room, and the handsomely equipped gymnasium with an athletic instructor in constant attendance.

From there the merry troupe proceeded to the extensive kitchens where the food was prepared, and on to the big refrigeration room where huge sides of beef and many other varieties of meat and vegetables were preserved.

They even went deep into the hold of the ship to the boiler room where they watched the huge engines which propelled the *Triton* through the water.

When the tour was completed Ray, Ros and Tom separated from the group and went to the sport deck where they had several lively games of deck tennis. Tiring of that after awhile, they hurried to their cabins, and returned with their baseball equipment and proceeded to have a catch.

The *Triton* rolled in the heavy sea swells, tilting first to port, then to starboard, and it made catching and throwing a baseball a little difficult. Several times one of the boys would miss a toss and then have to scurry after the bounding ball to keep it from going into the ocean.

Sunday and Monday passed quickly on board ship. The boys were continually active. Monday morning the entire All-Star team went swimming in the pool. All noticed how much warmer it was getting now that they were going farther south. In the afternoon Jimmy Ames and Clyde Mallory ran their charges through light calisthenic drills to keep their muscles limbered up. They occupied themselves tossing a baseball around, then Tom and Bart were taken aside to pitch to Dressen to take the kinks out of their arms.

By this time Tom's injured leg was almost completely healed and he only experienced a slight twinge of pain when he put his weight on the foot. As for Ray, his ankle had healed nicely. The only thing he missed was the opportunity to obtain some batting practice. He was very much afraid he might become rusty after several days lay-off. However, there was nothing to be done until they were on dry land again.

On Monday evening, the night before the *Triton* was due to dock in Havana, the sea turned rough. The night was cloudy and a stiff breeze sprang up, churning the blue Caribbean into dark, heaving swells. Several of the regular passengers failed to appear in the dining room for the evening meal and even Tom began to feel a little seasick so that he retired to the cabin shared by the three chums about eight o'clock.

Ray and Ros braved the elements and took several turns about the promenade deck.

"That water looks plenty rough," observed Ray, watching the ship plunge down into a deep trough, then climb to the crest of a long, rolling comber.

"And not nearly as inviting as it did this afternoon," murmured Ros.

"Tomorrow we'll be in Havana."

"And I'll be glad to plant my feet on firm ground

again. This constant rocking and pitching is giving me sea legs."

At nine o'clock Ray suggested that they go into the promenade lounge and listen to the seven-piece string orchestra that was playing for the guests. They entered the lounge and found it practically deserted, save for a few people scattered here and there in big soft chairs.

They found a sofa and took seats, their eyes drawn to the stout, imperious looking woman sitting in an armchair not far from the entrance to the lounge.

"Will you look at the string of pearls about that woman's neck," said Ros suddenly. He spoke with awe and his eyes were wide with admiration.

"They must be worth plenty of money," said Ray.

"I'd be afraid to wear anything like that for fear of losing them or having them stolen."

Ray nodded, his attention attracted by a slender, sallow-faced man with a long aquiline nose and dark beady eyes. He was dressed immaculately in tuxedo trousers and white waistcoat, but there was a hard look about his face. His mouth was thin and not pleasant to look at.

"There's a tough customer, if you ask me," said Ray.

Ros followed Ray's gaze and murmured, "He sure is. Maybe he's a gangster."

"And after that woman's string of pearls," added Ray.

Ros laughed. "Maybe we ought to be detectives.

Wouldn't it be funny if he turned out to be a Sunday school teacher."

"That would be funny." Ray broke off and gestured. "There's Lacey, the steward that showed us around the *Triton*."

Both boys watched the steward, carrying a small metal tray in his hand, move along the opposite side of the lounge, then cross over in front of the orchestra. He was about to pass the swarthy looking man by the door when the latter made a half turn and appeared to say something out of the side of his mouth.

Lacey gave a surprised start and almost dropped the tray, glanced swiftly at the man, then hurried off, his pace definitely faster than it had been.

"Say, that was a queer one," observed Ray. "Didn't it look to you as if that fellow said something to Lacey."

"It sure did." Ros' face was serious and his eyelids narrowed slightly. "Lacey looked startled—as if he knew the fellow—yet didn't want to talk to him."

"Maybe we're beginning to imagine things," said Ray with a laugh. "We've got too much time on our hands."

Suddenly the orchestra began playing another tune and the two boys saw the swarthy man turn his back on them and move out of the lounge. Suddenly the lights went out and the lounge was plunged into Stygian blackness.

"Where's the lights?" yelled Ros.

Somewhere a woman screamed in fright. At the other end of the lounge another woman screamed. The orchestra stopped playing, and Ros and Ray lunged to their feet as another cry issued from a spot near the orchestra platform.

"Help! My necklace! I've been robbed!"

"It's that woman!" cried Ray. "Maybe that dark fellow tried to rob her."

They plunged ahead through the room, stumbling over chairs, and rolling with the motion of the ship. They saw a darker blot in front of them that was the figure of a man. It turned and moved off into a spot of illumination in the corridor giving exit from the lounge. Both boys caught a glimpse of a white waistcoat.

"After him!" yelled Ray.

"I'm with you," said Ros and followed Ray's mad dash from the lounge.

They collided with several members of the orchestra scrambling down from the platform. The woman was still screaming shrilly. Outside on the promenade deck there was a hurried scuffle of feet as others were attracted by the commotion.

Ray and Ros plunged into the half-gloom of an inner corridor and swung left toward the door leading to the outer deck. As they stepped outside and looked aft along the heaving deck, there was a loud clatter and they heard a man shout angrily: "Why don't you watch where you're going?"

"Come on!" said Ray. "He must have gone that way."

Ray and Ros raced along the deck. As they approached the end of the glassed-in portion of the promenade, they noticed an elderly gray-haired man getting to his feet and brushing off his clothes. The man turned and stared unbelievingly at them as they raced past and out to the open air.

"Crazy people. Racing around the boat," grumbled the man.

Behind the two boys who were intent on catching the running figure they suspected was the thief, there lifted a great clamor of sound. People ran back and forth. Somewhere a woman was still screaming.

Out in the tangy, wet air, Ray turned to the narrow stairway that led to the boat deck above.

"He may have gone up here," said Ray in a husky whisper.

"Well, go on. I'm right behind you," urged Ros.

CHAPTER XV

A STRANGE ADVENTURE

THE two friends reached the boat deck and sped along the dark expanse of this upper level of the *Triton*. A long line of lifeboats appeared on their left. suddenly out of the corner of his eye, Ray detected a glimpse of white.

"Wait!" he called to Ros and spun on his heel, intent on going back to the lifeboat he had just passed.

As he turned the tarpaulin covering one of the boats lifted and a tall figure leaped out and ran toward the stairway. But Ray was very fleet. He raced after the flying figure and then with a desperate lunge, flung himself headlong at that running shape before him.

Catapulting through the air, Ray's arms closed around the man's body, slid down behind the knees and dropped the man in his tracks.

Immediately Ray found himself in a furious rough-and-tumble fight. The man beneath him squirmed free and rammed a hard fist against his cheek. Ros plunged in with a wild yell and with Ray's help tried to pin the fellow down.

In the dark neither boy could distinguish the fea-

tures of their adversary. The man's breath came hard
and labored as he struggled against the uneven odds.
Suddenly Ray uttered a gasp of pain as the man's feet
shot out and caught him in the pit of the stomach, hurling him against a low ventilator pipe.

He was dazed and weak and the breath had been
knocked out of him. For a moment he watched that
darker blot on the deck that was Ros and the unknown
man, wrestling about. Then Ray saw Ros roll over
from a savage blow and the other man prepared to
get up.

Somehow Ray rallied his energy, got to his feet and
brought the man to his knees with another vicious
tackle. But the latter whirled as Ray scrambled on
top of him and drove a knuckled fist full into Ray's
face, snapping his teeth together.

Ros tried to get back into the fight, but was tripped
by the threshing legs of Ray and his assailant and fell
flat on his face. Ray, however, pumped a hard right to
the pale orb that was his opponent's features. For a
moment they traded punches savagely and Ros contrived to come back and help Ray.

Yet, the other man was powerful and wiry. He
squirmed free of their constraining bodies. The heel of
one shoe tagged Ros' chin and sent him crashing to the
deck. Then Ray and the man got to their feet and
slugged toe to toe.

Ray took a wicked right under the heart and another

right to the chin before rushing in with a stiff jab to the other man's mouth. Dimly he caught the motion of the man's arm descending in an arc above his head. It was almost pitch black up here on the boat deck, but Ray noted that there was some slender dark object in the man's hand.

Frantically the boy tried to duck, while driving home a wild left. He felt his fist strike bone and flesh, then something hard grazed the side of his head and he staggered backward. He swayed dizzily, his head throbbing with pain, then fell forward.

For a moment or two lights swam before his eyes. Dimly he heard the pound of retreating footsteps and realized he and Ros had lost their quarry. He fought back the pain in his head.

"Ros!" he called.

"Here," answered a voice close at hand.

Ray stirred and saw a dark blot take shape a few yards away and move toward him.

"You all right?" demanded Ray.

"Except for an aching jaw, I'm all in one piece," responded Ros.

Ray pushed to his hands and knees and suddenly his groping fingers encountered something hard and smooth and round.

"I've got them!" he shouted.

"What have you got?" demanded Ros, now close at hand in the gloom.

"The pearls! At least, it feels like them. Yes, it's a string of round objects. Maybe the thief dropped them in the scuffle."

Excitement crept into Ros' voice. "Let's get to some light and see."

Ray pulled himself to his feet and groaned. "Boy, I wonder what that fellow hit me with. My head feels like a balloon."

"Probably a blackjack."

Together the two chums swayed to the stairway and clattered down to the promenade deck. They moved to the first light set in the ceiling of the enclosed portion of the deck.

"It *is* the pearls!" ejaculated Ray.

"What a break!" breathed Ros.

"Too bad we couldn't hold on to that fellow."

"Got any idea who he was? It was so dark I couldn't see his face."

Ray shook his head. "Must have been that suave looking fellow we saw standing near the orchestra platform." Then Ray's eyes narrowed and an odd expression illumined them. "I wonder if it could have been Lacey. The thief was wearing a white waistcoat and I remember Lacey walked out of the lounge just before that happened."

"I don't think he'd do anything like that," said Ros.

"Guess you're right. Well, we'd better get back to the lounge and report our find. The captain will probably be there."

Not only was Captain Morton Blaine in the lounge, but there was a host of passengers, stewards and other ship employees crowded in the room. All eyes were fastened on the stout, regal looking woman who was moaning her loss while Captain Blaine tried to comfort her.

"My pearls! They're gone!" wailed the woman, tears streaming down her cheeks. "They're worth a fortune. It's terrible. My husband gave them to me as a wedding anniversary gift. He'll be furious because he hadn't had time to insure them."

"You say the lights went out suddenly and then someone tore the string of pearls from your neck?" inquired the captain.

"Yes! Yes! Can't you do something? Find the man!"

"Oh, Captain Blaine, we've got the pearls!" shouted Ray, pushing forward through the throng. Now Ray also saw Jimmy Ames and several of the other All-Stars who were interested spectators.

The captain looked startled. "Where did you find them?"

Quickly Ray gave an account of their chase which had led to the boat deck and the furious struggle which had ensued.

"I guess the pearls must have slipped out of the fellow's pocket during the fight," concluded the boy.

"That was fine work."

"Oh, I'm so glad you boys found them!" exclaimed

the woman, drying her eyes. "I must reward you. They were worth more than money alone to me. It was the sentiment behind them."

"It was nothing," said Ray. "We don't want anything."

"We're just sorry the thief got away from us."

"Any idea who it was?" queried Blaine.

Ray and Ros explained their suspicions, but did not bring Lacey's name into the discussion. Blaine turned to several of the stewards and asked them if they recalled seeing anyone answering to the description of the swarthy looking man Ray and Ros had seen lingering around the orchestra platform in the lounge. They all answered in the negative.

"Well, I don't suppose it would do any good if you had seen the man's face. He would deny it now. However, we'll keep a sharp watch for any future happenings of this type." He turned to one of the stewards. "Call the Chief Steward to my room on the bridge. I have some orders for him regarding the safety of our passengers."

The steward departed and then the captain set about accompanying the regal looking woman to her stateroom. Slowly the crowd dispersed, and Jimmy Ames and the rest of the players closed in on Ros and Ray.

"Looks like you fellows had a nice little adventure," said Ames with a grin.

"Hail, the hero!" grunted Himber with a smile. But

Ray glancing at the Springfield athlete noted that he was smiling with his lips, not with his eyes.

"Wish I had been in on that fight," said Bill Scully of St. Luke's.

"You can have my aching head," said Ray with a wry grin.

"Well," suggested Ames dryly, "I'd advise all of you to turn in and get some sleep. We've got a big day ahead of us tomorrow. We'll be making a tour of Havana in the morning and in the afternoon we'll get some practice. Don't forget I want you fellows in good shape for those Cubans."

With the Clarkville coach's warning ringing in their ears, the boys soon scattered and went to their cabins. Ray and Ros drew apart still discussing the identity of the mysterious thief.

"Thought you might say something to Blaine about Lacey," remarked Ros.

Ray answered seriously. "No sense involving him because we're not even sure he was the thief." Fifty feet away from them a white-coated figure strode along the deck and disappeared into a narrow passageway. "Say, wasn't that Lacey?"

Ros glanced up. "That did look like him."

"And if I'm not mistaken he had a black eye," snapped Ray. "Come on. Maybe he was the thief after all."

The boys broke into a run along the deck, scampered

through the passageway, crossed to the starboard side of the promenade, but saw no one.

"Let's prowl around on the boat deck again," Ray urged.

"Sure. Maybe we'll find something."

Accordingly, they moved along the deck, stepping outside into the cool air. The sea was running full and heavy, and thick clouds scudded across the warm, tropical sky. They reached the stairway and climbed it stealthily. Shadows ebbed and flowed all about them.

"Kind of spooky up here," observed Ros in an undertone.

Ray held up his hand. "Wait! I think I heard voices." He pointed with his hand toward the line of lifeboats near the rail. "Let's get closer."

Crouching low, they moved forward through the gloom, the murmur of conversation reaching them more distinctly now. Tension gripped their muscles. Their eyes were distended, straining to pierce the gloom. They came up against one of the lifeboats and paused there, hearing one of those strange voices lift angrily.

"You bungled that job tonight."

"I couldn't help it," said another voice, a note of fear chilling the tone. "I never expected those boys to follow me and—"

"Shut up. So you let a pair of teen age kids get the best of you." There was a pause while an ominous menace oiled the first man's voice. "Or maybe you did it

on purpose. Maybe you're figuring on double-crossin'
me an' the boys?"

"That wasn't it at all."

"No? Well, it better not happen again."

"It won't."

Ray turned to Ros and whispered: "Doesn't that
second voice sound like Lacey's?"

"Come to think of it, it does. I wonder——"

"Easy——I don't want to miss what they're saying."

The first man was talking, an arrogant hardness
clipping the words past his lips.

"You'll answer for this. Those pearls were worth
plenty."

"I'll answer for nothing. I'm through." There was
defiance in the other man's tone. Defiance and something akin to desperate fear. "I'm quitting. I've had
enough of this stealing, of hiding from the law. For
what? You promised me——"

"So you're goin' to quit, are you?" snarled the first
man. "I figured you were yellow. Well, get this, we're
not lettin' you quit to have you spill the beans to the
cops."

"You can't stop me."

"No? You're through, Lacey!"

Ray whispered excitedly. "Ros, it is Lacey! He
must be in with a gang of crooks!"

The first man was talking. "They'll never find you
in the sea."

There was the sudden sharp sound of a scuffle. Some-one uttered a low cry of pain.

"There's trouble!" said Ray and started around the lifeboat.

Again there was a muffled outcry. It was followed by the solid impact of a knuckled fist meeting flesh and bone. Then a split second later there was a dull splash, as if a heavy body had hurtled into the ocean.

Ray raced to the rail and a slinking figure darted past him. He lunged at the man, got his hands on the latter's coat, then lost his hold. But he kept on, not caring about that escaping figure. He ran along the rail, eyes scanning the foaming wake of the *Triton*.

"There's someone in the water, Ros!" he shouted.

"Maybe it's Lacey!"

"I'm going after him," snapped Ray and ripped off his shoes without bothering to unlace them.

"You'd better not. It's rough."

"Can't be helped. You sound the alarm. Stop the ship!"

With that terse warning, Ray clambered to the top of the rail, got to his feet and poised there with the damp sea air whipping spray into his face. The roll-ing combers looked dark and forbidding, but he hesi-tated only long enough to make sure that his plunge would carry him away from the side of the *Triton*. The next moment his rangy frame was a dark blur, jack-knifing toward the churning waves.

CHAPTER XVI

MAN OVERBOARD

WITH hammering heart catapulting into his throat, Ros stood at the rail of the heaving cruise ship, watching his chum dive into the ominous black pall of the Caribbean. He saw him drop far beneath the waves. Afterward, a round head broke the surface and paddled furiously toward a dimly bobbing figure in the distance.

Swiftly Ros turned on his heel and raced down to the promenade.

"Man overboard!" he cried. "Stop the ship!"

People gathered quickly, attracted by his shouts for help. A bell clanged on the ship. Stewards ran back and forth. An officer from the bridge appeared and Ros told him tersely what had happened. The officer ran off. Again a bell clanged and the huge engines of the *Triton* began to churn in reverse while sailors sped to the boat deck to lower a lifeboat.

Out in the brackish waters of the Caribbean Ray felt himself submerged in a veritable flood. The sea appeared to suck him down to frigid depths. His lungs were straining with the pressure of air, demanding release. Then suddenly he shot to the surface, gasping in the fresh air in great gulps.

A rolling comber crashed over him. Sea water entered his mouth, found its way down his throat and set him to coughing. He bobbed around on the crest of a wave like a bouncing cork. Then he saw the blurred shape of that other man. He saw the man strike out at the water feebly with weak arms, then go under as a black wave cascaded over him.

Ray kicked out savagely with his feet, his arms cutting through the water with a smooth rapidity. He plunged through a deep swell, fighting the pull of the strong tide. Already the *Triton* was some distance away, but the foaming wake hit him and spun him around like a piece of dry driftwood. He saw that figure bob to the surface, then sink out of sight beneath a rolling comber.

Hope was beginning to die within Ray, but he made one last effort. He put all the power in his shoulders and arms into another half dozen strokes. He shot like a torpedo through the waves, his clawing fingers suddenly contacting cloth and flesh.

A groping arm circled his neck as the drowning man fought for a grip on him. The man was almost out, yet some desperate force within him, impelled him to hang on. Ray had to hit the man in the jaw, then flip him over on his back. Using an across-the-chest carry, Ray started to swim toward the distant shape of the *Triton*.

This was John Lacey he had rescued. As he had come up close to the figure of the man, and the latter had attempted to strangle him in his attempt to hang on, Ray had secured a clear look at the white, bruised face of the steward.

But now the only thought that throbbed through Ray was this: Would Ros be able to give the alarm in time to stop the *Triton* and have a lifeboat sent out? As a rolling wave carried them to its crest, he glimpsed the ship swinging about in a distant trough. But he saw no lifeboat!

Tides of warning threaded Ray's tingling nerves. A growing fear put its clawing pressure about his throat. It was a tightening hand that threatened to choke the air out of his body. His arms were tiring. His legs were tiring. Every muscle in his sinewy frame cried out for release from this terrible effort. Things were beginning to swim before his eyes—the distant shape of the *Triton*, the rolling combers, the dark sky filled with fleecy white clouds whipped by a roving wind. His movements became mechanical. Lacey was like some dead weight seeking to pull him to the ocean floor. Waves crashed over him, doused him with salty spray, stung his narrow-lidded eyes.

How long he fought the raging sea, he did not know. Consciousness must have left him momentarily, for he fought up out of the numbing black void to find one of the *Triton's* lifeboats, riding the rolling waves at his side. They had pulled Lacey into the boat and now they were hauling him out of the sea.

"Easy does it, lad," cautioned one of the sailors. "You'll be all right now."

Somehow Ray managed to whisper. "Is—is he all right?"

"Got a pile of water in his lungs but he'll pull out of it."

Someone propped an arm under Ray's head and tipped the neck of a narrow bottle to his lips. Abruptly a hot, fiery liquid coursed down his throat. It made him cough and gag for breath, but it brought instant heat and warmth to his chilled body.

It took more than ten minutes to row back to the *Triton* which had put about to await the return of the lifeboat. At last, the boat was lifted to its perch on the boat deck and Ray and Lacey were rushed to a roomy suite of cabins fitted out like a small infirmary.

A doctor moved briskly around Lacey. Ray was obliged to strip and take a hot shower, then wrap himself in blankets. The same was done for Lacey after he had been treated for immersion. Ray was little the worse for wear when Captain Blaine appeared with Ros and Jimmy Ames and several of the ship's officers to question him.

Ray told his story of hearing the scuffle on the boat deck, omitting his and Ros' recognition of Lacey's voice and that part of the conversation the two boys had overheard.

"Let's have your version of this affair," requested the captain, turning his attention to Lacey.

The steward reddened and his voice was husky. "It was mighty strange, sir," he said after a brief pause, during which he shot a quick, agonized glance at Ray. "I went up on the boat deck for a breath of air and I was leaning over the rail, looking out at the water, when someone attacked me from the rear."

"Did the person say anything?" demanded Blaine, his glance skeptical.

Lacey hesitated. "Yes—something about 'I've got you now and you'll pay.' "

"And then?"

"Well, I turned to fight the fellow. We struggled a moment, and then a heavy object hit me along the side of the head. Next thing I remember was hitting the water."

Blaine nodded somberly. "You were hit by a blunt object. The doctor says it was probably a blackjack. I notice you have a puffed lip and a swollen eye. You get that in the same fight?"

"I—I guess so." Lacey's gaze darted in guilty fashion toward Ray and Ros.

When asked if he could identify his attacker, Lacey replied in the negative, giving as an excuse the fact that it had been too dark on the boat deck to distinguish the features of the man.

Blaine appeared to be visibly disturbed. "I don't like it. Twice in one night there is trouble on the ship."

"If I may so, sir," offered Lacey, "perhaps the party who attacked me mistook me for someone else."

"No doubt," agreed Blaine tersely. "This must be

stopped. I am glad we dock in the morning. It is too late now to check on the passenger list but we'll keep a sharp watch for trouble. As for you—" Blaine faced Ray and a smile broke the strict composure of his features. "I want to thank you for what you've done to-night. Twice you have put myself and the *Triton's* officers in your debt. But now I think you ought to have some rest."

"I agree with you, captain," broke in Ames with a grin, "and I aim to see that he gets to bed right this minute. Come along, Ray."

Ray turned to Ames and smiled at Ros who had been an interested witness of the proceedings. On the way to their stateroom, Ames remarked:

"Well, I hope this ends your adventures, Ray."

"I guess I've had enough for awhile."

"I want you to be more careful," said Ames seriously. "Of course, I'm proud of what you've done, but you must remember Clarkville and myself are responsible for your own safety. I wouldn't want anything to happen to you. Besides, you must be in shape for the All-Star game."

Ray laughed. "I'm ready to play nine innings right now."

"And so am I," added Ros.

"You boys only think you are," said Ames as they reached the boys' stateroom and entered.

Ames stopped a moment to inquire of Tom how he

was feeling. It developed that the Clarkville pitcher was much better and had been sleeping during all the excitement. Accordingly, with another warning that Ray and Ros should go right to bed, the Light and Dark Blue mentor departed.

In a twinkling with Ray and Ros eagerly interrupting one another, Tom was informed of all that had transpired up on deck. Tom whistled in amazement when they had finished.

"And to think I had to sleep all through that. I *would* miss the fun."

"It wasn't all fun," protested Ros, rubbing his aching jaw with the palm of his hand. "My chin still feels as if a mule kicked me."

Ray started to undress and had to stifle a yawn. "Boy, I really am tired."

"You should be," grunted Tom.

Fifteen minutes later Ray and Ros climbed into their bunks and prepared to turn out the light. Suddenly a light tap sounded on the door. Ray rose to a sitting position, throwing back the sheets.

"Who is it?" he queried.

There was no answer. After a moment's silence the knock was repeated.

"Better see who it is," directed Tom.

Ray grunted, heaved himself out of bed and padded to the door. He gave a surprised start when he saw Lacey standing in the shadows.

"Can I come in?" asked the steward. He cast a hasty glance up and down the corridor. "Sorry to disturb you boys but I must talk to you."

"Come on in," invited Ray a trifle grimly. "I've been wanting to talk to you, too."

Lacey entered and Ray closed the portal softly after him. The steward looked white and haggard and his face was bruised. Now he ventured a quizzical glance at Ray.

"What do you mean?" husked Lacey.

Ros now joined Ray and soon Tom hopped out of his bunk to join them.

"I think you owe us an explanation," said Ray. He gestured to Ros. "My friend and I overheard your conversation—part of it, at least—with some man up on the boat deck. He threatened you and before we could intervene you were overboard."

"Yes, and I noticed you didn't mention that in your story to the captain," added Ros grimly. "Why?"

Lacey was definitely upset. His mouth worked nervously and his eyes were clouded with fear and despair. It was evident he had gone through some great ordeal this night.

"I'll try to explain," he said.

"You'd better," replied Ray. "And while you're talking, you might tell us what you know about that woman's necklace!"

The shock of Ray's words hit the steward like a

bullet. He took a step backward and all blood drained from his cheeks.

"You know about that?" he whispered.

"We're guessing," admitted Ros, "but we don't think we're wrong."

"What is this all about?" demanded Tom, bewildered. "You chaps are far ahead of me."

"Just listen and you'll find out," said Ray. He turned to Lacey once more. "All right. We're waiting."

Lacey began slowly and with obvious effort, conscious all the while of the sharp stares directed at him by the three boys. However, after a moment it spilled from his lips in a torrent of anguish.

It was a pathetic story. Lacey was an only son supporting a widowed mother. Several months ago his mother had been taken ill. Her condition grew more serious. Doctors told him an operation was the only thing that would save her life. But there was the question of money and his mother was too proud to go as a charity case.

Then on one of the trips to Havana, Lacey had served a suave, dark-looking man. One night they had gotten into a conversation. Somehow Lacey told his story and the other man, eyes glinting strangely, began talking of money to be made easily.

At first, Lacey had objected. Earning that money meant stepping beyond the law. It was risky, fraught with peril. But the other man had talked smoothly. The temptation was great. The need was greater. His mother's life! And so he had joined this syndicate of thieves operating on cruise ships, stealing jewelry and disposing of it in the West Indies or back in New York months later, after the incident had been forgotten.

But the gang had double-crossed Lacey. He had stolen a diamond bracelet and had been promised a huge sum as his share. It would have proved enough for his mother's operation. The syndicate kept stalling him off. Then his mother had died. Now he was sick of it all and he wanted to pull out, but they wouldn't let him.

The three boys were shocked by this story. They looked at one another in startled amazement. True, the story sounded fantastic, but one glance at the impassioned look on Lacey's features told them he was telling the truth. At the end he broke down and was near to tears.

"Promise me you won't tell Captain Blaine or the police. I'd lose my job and go to jail," moaned Lacey.

"I guess you would," agreed Ray. "And you stole that necklace tonight?"

"Yes. The gang leader forced me to do it. Threatened me if I failed to get it."

Ray was puzzled. "I don't know what to say. You did wrong. That much is certain."

"I was a fool," admitted Lacey. "I don't know what made me do it. And Mother died in spite of it all."

"I guess you've learned your lesson. We won't say anything. All right with you, Ros?"

"Sure," said Ros. "Besides, the woman got her necklace back tonight."

"But can't you expose the gang?" demanded Ray. "Who is behind it?"

"Jan Straber is his name but it would be no use," said Lacey. "If I talk I'll implicate myself. Besides, I have no proof. And if I try to have them arrested they'll only try to get me."

"But surely something can be done," protested Ros.

"I wish I knew," said Lacey, distress pulling at the corners of his mouth. "I'm afraid Straber thinks I will talk now that he knows I won't work for him any more. He'll be after me."

Ray was thoughtful a moment. "That certainly ties our hands. Only thing you can do I guess is wait till you get back to New York, then try to get another job where you won't be apt to meet Straber."

"And in the meantime?"

"Why not stay with us?" asked Ros. "We'll be touring Havana in the morning. If you can get shore leave, join us."

Lacey's face lit up. "I will. Thanks. I only hope it works. Straber is clever. He is an artist at make-up and disguise, and if we see him tomorrow in Havana we might not even know him.   It's a desperate gang.   They play for high stakes and sometimes they don't care how they get what they want."

"You get shore leave," advised Ray, "and stick with our team.   They won't dare try anything with so many fellows around."

Gratitude put color back in Lacey's cheeks.   He thanked them over and over again before slipping out of their stateroom and vanishing down the shadowy corridor.

CHAPTER XVII

DANGER AT NIGHT

EARLY the next morning the *Triton* anchored within sight of the famous Morro Castle, and passengers soon began going ashore in small power launches. Some passengers lingered on the promenade deck, tossing dimes and quarters to grinning native boys who would dive quickly below the surface to retrieve the coins and then bob up again, after sticking the money in their mouths.

With considerable difficulty Jimmy Ames and Clyde Mallory rounded up their charges, and hired four open touring cars of ancient vintage to take them on a short tour around the city. John Lacey had induced Captain Blaine to grant him shore leave, so the steward joined the party, piling into the car with Ray, Ros and Tom.

"Say, these Cuban drivers sure do take chances," observed Ros after they had shot across an important intersection without even slowing down, and had narrowly missed crashing into another open car filled with gaping tourists.

"If we live to play those Cuban All-Stars we'll be lucky," said Ray with a shaky laugh.

It was true. The nonchalant chauffeur of their car seemed to rely more on his horn than on his brakes. Whenever he reached an intersection, he would sound the horn and step on the accelerator.

The sky was a deep blue and the heat was almost as intense as mid-summer in New York. Everywhere men walked in white suits. The boys saw a profusion of royal palms, full-blooming red hibiscus and other tropical flowers.

Their first visit was to the Capitolio or capitol of Cuba, a magnificent structure which Cubans say required the unceasing toil of five thousand men, working day and night in three eight-hour shifts, for four and a half years. It is built of marble from the Isle of Pines and cost seventeen million dollars.

The boys were awed by the unusual appointments inside the building—the beautiful hand-carved mahogany furniture, the solid marble floor in the main hall beneath a dome which is eighteen feet higher than the dome in the capitol building in Washington, D. C., and the 24-carat Kimberly diamond set in the marble floor to mark the zero point of all distances in Cuba.

Later they journeyed to the Corona cigar factory which covers an entire block. The guide explained to them that Havana has the largest cigar factories in the world. From there they went to the Cabana Fortress and El Morro Castle. Afterward, they took a ride through beautiful suburban sections, coming back to the city to alight from the cars so they could mingle with the colorful crowds gathered in the streets.

After lunch they took a bus to the baseball field and Coaches Ames and Mallory held a two-hour workout. Tom and Bart Himber limbered up their arms, tossing balls to Fred Dressen, while the entire team went through an intensive batting drill. Ray proved to the All-Star coaches that he hadn't lost his batting eye by poling several long flies over the distant right field barrier.

Then, in the evening an arrangement was made to take a drive out through the suburbs, stopping off to watch some of Havana's famous jai-alai games—a game similar to handball in which the players wear a long basket-like cover on their hand and extending halfway up their arm, by means of which they catch the ball and smash it back against the distant hard wall.

Four cars with native drivers were hired and the boys teamed up, Ray, Ros, Tom and Bill Scully, the third baseman from St. Luke's getting in the same car. Again the automobiles were the old-fashioned open touring cars. There was a lot of joking back and forth between cars, and Ames and Mallory had trouble in seeing that everyone was accounted for on the All-Stars. They were about to pull away from the hotel when Ray suddenly grasped Ros' arm.

"Ros! See those two fellows under that tree across the street?"

Ros glanced in the direction Ray indicated. "Yeah. What about them?"

"I've been watching them the past few minutes and they sure have been interested in what we're doing. They look suspicious."

Tom broke in with an amused laugh. "Got the jitters, Ray?"

"Of course not," retorted Ray.

"Think it's some of that chap Straber's hired men on the lookout for Lacey?"

"You never can tell," said Ray seriously.

"Well, they can spend all night looking for Lacey in our crowd without having any luck," grunted Ros.

At the last moment Lacey had been obliged to forego this excursion with Ray and his chums when Captain Blaine had cancelled his shore leave. Of course, the boys were disappointed, since Lacey would have been a valuable guide on their night tour of Havana. However, Lacey's absence did not dim their ardor for the trip.

"It's too bad Lacey couldn't come along," murmured Ray absently, his eyes searching the shadowy gloom across the wide street, shaded by big royal palms.

The two men were still there. Dressed in dark suits, light Panama hats pulled down over their eyes, they still watched the group in front of the hotel. The ruby eye of a cigarette made its crimson arc through the gloom as one of the men tossed the remains of his smoke in the street.

Ray's attention was taken away by the approach of Ames, making a final check-up on his charges.

"Everybody ready?" Ames asked.

"Let's go!" was the enthusiastic reply.

"All right. The drivers have instructions to stay close together. You fellows will bring up the rear."

Two tall, broad-shouldered boys who had been lingering in front of the hotel, now suddenly stepped into the touring car which was parked in front of the friends' vehicle.

"There go your Springfield friends, Himber and Dressen," said Tom to Ray, nudging the latter in the ribs. "I'm surprised you haven't had any trouble with them."

"We've been steering clear of each other, that's all," replied Ray.

A joyous shout lifted from the first automobile as it pulled away from the curb with a loud clashing of gears. The second followed it, then the car in which Himber and Dressen were riding, and finally the three chums' car.

Again they had the same unhappy experience of being terrorized by the careless, horn-honking type of driving which had characterized their morning tour of Havana. At every corner the heart of each boy leaped into his mouth as the bland native chauffeurs calmly tooted their horns and breezed across the intersections, somehow escaping collisions.

For a time they cruised along wide boulevards that

swept past the dark blue bay, sparkling under a tropical moon. Stars made a milky brilliance in the soft black canopy of sky overhead, and the breeze drifting inland across the water was light and warm, scented with the delicate fragrance of night-blooming jasmine.

"This is the life," said Ros, sinking back against the stiff leather cushion in the back seat.

"Nothing to do but take it easy," added Tom. "I'm beginning to see why people like to visit the tropics and why they hate to leave once they get there."

"I wonder what the fellows back at Clarkville are doing now," said Ray dreamily.

"Probably busy doing their assignments," was Ros' opinion.

"Good old Bert is having his second supper over in the cafeteria by this time," said Tom with a laugh.

The cars were leaving the quiet, beautiful residential section of the city. Now they were threading through dark, shadowy streets which were barely wide enough to admit the passage of two cars. The houses were built quite close to the street and the boys could glance right into the front rooms of the meager dwellings of Havana's poorer citizens.

A hundred yards ahead of them the first two cars executed a sharp right turn into another narrow thoroughfare, horns blaring loudly. Suddenly another horn shattered the stillness and a sleek, dark roadster shot past the car in which Ray and his chums were passengers.

Ray had a brief glimpse of two hard-looking men crouched behind the windshield, and a sudden sense of dread clamped its icy fingers around his heart. Motor roaring, the roadster jounced ahead, came abreast of the vehicle in which Himber and Dressen were riding with two other lads.

Without warning the driver of the roadster swerved his car toward the open touring car. The driver of the latter shouted angrily, spun his wheel, the ancient vehicle jumping the curb and bouncing dangerously close to the shabby dwellings which lined the thoroughfare.

"Look at that!" yelled Ray.

"Why that chap in the roadster is deliberately swerving into Himber's car," observed Ros.

"Don't you see?" demanded Ray. "It must be Straber's men. They're after—"

"You mean—Himber?"

"Yes!" shouted Ray. "Don't you remember? We both noticed how much alike Himber and Lacey looked. Those fellows probably think Himber is Lacey and they're out to get him."

"Good night!"

"Driver!" yelled Ray. "Hurry up! Step on the gas! Look at those cars!"

The Cuban chauffeur uttered a cry of fright and jammed on his brakes, turning a startled face toward the three chums and Bill Scully, all of them standing up in the rear.

Pandemonium was breaking loose up ahead. The

roadster slithered across the street and rammed the touring car. There was a splintering crash of smashed fenders, then before Ray's startled eyes, the two men leaped out of the roadster and hopped to the running board of the touring car.

Instantly the two men piled inside. Someone yelled. There was a cry of pain. Himber and Dressen stood up. One of the men clubbed Dressen with a wild right and the latter toppled backward, spilling the two boys in back of him. All three crashed to the floor of their car in a threshing tangle of arms and legs.

"Come on! They need help!" yelled Ray and leaped out of the car. Ros and Tom and Bill were right at his heels, sprinting down the narrow street in a wild dash to throw their combined strength against the two desperadoes attacking Bart Himber.

The chauffeur of the latter's vehicle had vaulted from his seat and was running for his life, yelling and screaming for the police.

"Give it to them, Bart!" yelled Ray hoarsely.

But even as Ray cried, a gasp of dismay escaped his lips as he saw the two men overpower Himber. One of them struck him with a hard blunt object along the side of the head and he slumped weakly in their arms. Quickly they threw him into the roadster, hopped in themselves and prepared to make their getaway.

"Stop!" shrilled Ray, anger riding his nerves with cruel spurs.

The motor of the roadster leaped into a full-throated roar. The driver shot it into gear. There was another grinding clash of metal and the roadster shot down from the curb, tipped over on two wheels, hung there precariously as if it would topple over, then righted itself.

Ray flung himself at the rear bumper, got a hand-hold on the chromium guard and was dragged a few feet over the rutted pavement before he was forced to relinquish his hold. The roadster shot forward in a burst of blue exhaust smoke, its red tail lights winking mockingly at the frustrated boys.

"They've got Himber!" said Ray. "Come on. We're going back to the car. We'll follow."

All four boys retraced their steps, racing back the way they came.

"We'll never catch them in this old bus," Ros protested.

"It's worth a try," panted Ray. To the astonished driver, he said, "Get in. We want this car. Follow them!"

"No! No. No follow!" retorted the driver.

Ray turned to Tom and Bill Scully. "Take him," he directed, and leaped in behind the wheel, while Ros vaulted in on the other side.

Tom and Bill ganged up on the yelling driver, bearing him back against the wall of a dark building. Fists flew through the air. Feet pounded along the narrow sidewalk. Somewhere a policeman's whistle pierced the din as windows were thrown open and a crowd swiftly gathered.

Not waiting for the outcome of Tom and Bill's struggle with the chauffeur, Ray shot the old touring car into gear.

"Wait for us!" yelled Tom, leaving off the fight for a minute.

"No time. See you later!" shrilled Ray over his shoulder, though it is doubtful if either Tom or Bill heard him above the roar of the ancient vehicle's exhaust.

Four blocks away Ray glimpsed the ruby lights of the roadster as it swung into a side street. Recklessly, Ray flung the car from first into second and then into high gear. Not once did he stop for an intersection. Hand pressed down hard on the horn, foot riffling the accelerator, Ray sent the car hurtling through the gloomy streets. He thought with a grim smile of his own fears when the Cuban driver had passed similar crossings a short time ago. But now the risk had to be run.

They came to the corner where the roadster had turned right, and Ray swung the car into that street, the tires screeching their protest at the speed of the turn. Up on the sidewalk they went, then bouncing down into the street, with Ray's foot ramming the accelerator to the floor, the old car responding admirably to the call for speed.

"There they are!" exclaimed Ros, as they broke into a wider boulevard and picked out the bobbing red lights of a car in the distance.

"Hope we're not following the wrong one," murmured Ray.

"It's a chance we'll have to take," replied Ros tensely, his eyes narrowed as the warm breeze hit them full in the face.

On and on the two cars raced, the winding road taking them farther and farther into the country. Despite the fact that the roadster was a much newer car than the vehicle Ray was driving, the first car could not gain because of the sharp curves in the road.

They slithered around bends, skidding toward the edge of the highway, the trees dark and thick all about them, only the white glare of their headlights, breaking the monotony of thick foliage and black asphalt.

"Boy, this chase is taking us deeper and deeper into the country," said Ray.

"We'll be lucky if we ever find our way back again."

Ray's reply was utterly grim. "We'll be lucky if we can catch those birds and keep them from doing whatever they intend doing to Bart Himber."

The motor's hum was a loud roar in their ears. Tires, laboring under intense pressure and strain, screeched as the old touring car lurched around a bend, then catapulted ahead under a renewed burst of speed.

"Look out!" yelled Ros. "There they are! We're going to crash into them!"

CHAPTER XVIII

A DARING ESCAPE

COLD shock numbed Ray's nerves for a clock tick of time. His hands froze to the wheel. His muscles refused to move and his eyes went wide with fear. Death stared Ray and Ros in the face for one fleeting instant. Slithering around the sharp bend in the road, the rocketing touring car swept down upon the roadster which had slewed across the highway, completely blocking it.

The driver was clambering out from behind the wheel. Inexorably the touring car roared toward the roadster. They were going to crash full into the side of the streamlined two-seater. Then Ray sprang into action, red blood leaping in full riot through his veins. His right foot blazed down upon the brake pedal.

The wheels locked. The tires made a screeching sound as the car skidded perilously along the asphalt. They were slowing down but would they avoid a crack-up? That was the question hammering at the nerves of Ray and Ros. The latter tensed himself for the shock of impact.

They were fifty feet away, then forty, twenty, ten

and five and still they were moving. Ray wrenched
desperately at the wheel. The car lurched crazily
across the road. Again he flipped the wheel, a loud
explosion testifying to the fact that they had blown a
tire. There was a final, lingering crash of metal as
the two cars hooked fenders, then broke free, the touring car slithering off the road and ramming into a tree.

Ray and Ros were shaken up. The wheel had dug
into Ray's stomach, knocking the wind out of him.
For a moment he and Ros sat there dazed, trying to
clear their vision. At last, numbed muscles functioned
again and Ray jumped from the car—to run full tilt
into the blue barrel of a revolver held in the fist of a
snarling, dark-featured man.

"Put up your hands and don't move."

"Why, they're only a couple of kids," muttered the
hatchet-faced man with the long scar disfiguring one
cheek, who came up behind the man with the gun.

"Put down that gun," ordered Ray bravely. "You've
got a friend of ours and we mean to have him."

"Lacey's your pal, huh?"

"He isn't Lacey," protested Ros.

"Oh, no?" snarled the hatchet-faced man. "We'll
let Straber decide that."

"You fools!" erupted Ray angrily, blood flushing his
cheeks. "That fellow you've captured is Bart Himber.
He's a ball player—one of the scholastic All-Stars from
the United States. We're playing a team from Havana
tomorrow."

"Do you expect us to believe that?" retorted the desperado, a cruel leer, distorting his thin lips.

"Better take them along," said the other man. "If they're friends of Lacey, Straber may want to see them."

"You'd better leave us go," warned Ray savagely, his fists clenching, "or you'll get into trouble."

"See how we're worrying!" The hatchet-faced man laughed. It was a harsh, grating sound. It disturbed the two boys, filled them with a sudden sense of dread.

The other man waved his revolver toward the roadster.

"Move along. You're going to join your pal. Don't try any funny stuff or you'll get clubbed over the head."

With wild anger having its way with them, Ray and Ros permitted themselves to be marched to the roadster. Under the threat of the gun, they piled into the car, noting that Bart was still unconscious from the blow he had received on the head. There was a little blood on his scalp. A dark streak of it had dried along his right cheek and temple.

Ray's thoughts were bleak and dismal as the roadster lurched away, sped along the highway for another two miles, then went jouncing along a narrow side road, threading through a thick stand of timber. He and Ros and Bart were in a jam. These were desperate men. Ray felt a cold weight claw at him as he thought of the dire possibilities if even Straber should mistake Himber for Lacey. It was evident they wanted Lacey out of the way, but they had received instructions from their leader to bring Lacey to some hideout.

Tomorrow was the long looked-for baseball game, but at the moment Ray doubted if he'd ever again see the sunshine, or ever again feel the sharp tingle in his palms that came from a baseball that was well hit and destined for the distant fences.

After ten minutes of bumping and clattering over the rutted dirt road, they emerged upon a tiny clearing in the woods. Set back against the low-hanging trees was a small cabin. The roadster slid to a stop and the two boys were ordered out. Bart was hauled to his feet. He opened his eyes, swayed dizzily and was supported by the hatchet-faced man. In the rays of a flashlight held by the driver, he saw Ray and Ros.

"Where am I? What are you fellows doing here?"

"We're in a jam," ground out Ray.

"I'll say you are," grunted the driver with a brittle laugh.

Bart glanced around at his captors and returning memory narrowed his eyes in rage.

"I remember now. You snakes crowded us off the road, then jumped me. By gosh, you'll pay for that!" With a roar Bart clenched his fists and started forward, then stopped, a look of amazement and horror on his face as he saw the levelled revolver in the driver's fist.

"How do you feel now, Lacey?" queried the driver.

"Lacey?" whispered Bart, puzzled.

"Yeah Don't pretend you aren't Lacey."

"You're crazy!" protested Bart.

"Shut up and get inside. All of you!" roared the hatchet-faced man.

He kicked open the door of the cabin with his foot and thrust the three boys ahead of him into the gloom. The other renegade fumbled around in the shack, searching with the flashlight for a lamp. At last he found one and lighted it. It was a rude, one-room cabin with two bunks slapped against the wall on the south side.

"Better tie them up, Horton," said the driver to his partner.

Horton grunted and went outside to the car. He returned with some thin rope and hastily tied the wrists of all three boys behind their backs. Ray, his mind intent on gaining their release, regardless of the risk involved, contrived to spread his hands sidewise a trifle as the cords were knotted about his wrists.

"Straber ought to be along soon," grunted Horton.

"Before he comes, you'll both be in jail," warned Ray.

A derisive laugh greeted Ray's remark. Horton stepped outside for a moment and the other man went to the door, looking down the rutted road.

Bart looked at Ray and Ros, his face lined with strain and embarrassment.

"How did you fellows get here?" he asked.

In an undertone Ray quickly explained the events that had transpired, emphasizing the resemblance they had noticed between the *Triton's* steward and Bart.

Bart whistled. "That puts us in a fine fix." He grinned, then, and there was more comradeship in that gesture than Ray had ever seen the Springfield lad exhibit before. "I'm glad you fellows are with me—if you know what I mean. I guess I've been sort of—"

Bart broke off quickly as the driver, whom they had all heard called Brigham by the other man, stepped inside the cabin again. He flashed a hard look at the three boys but said nothing. In the meantime Ray was struggling with his bonds. He felt the cords bite deeply into his flesh and the pain almost nauseated him. But still he kept up the struggle, feeling them loosen a trifle after ten minutes of gruelling labor that brought the perspiration out on his forehead.

"We've got to make a break out of here," he hissed to Ros.

"But how?" asked his chum dismally.

"I'm getting the cords loose. When I get free, you shift around a bit so I can work on your bonds. Pass the word to Bart. After you're free, you work on Bart."

Several times both desperadoes strode into the cabin to see if the boys were still trussed up on the floor where they had been left. Once Horton said with a hard grin:

"Straber will be here soon. That ought to make you happy, Lacey."

When Horton went out Ray renewed his efforts

again. At last the rope gave. His wrists were raw, and the pain shot all the way up his arms but he finally got free. With circulation restored in his hands and arms, Ray toiled away at Ros' bonds.

"Hurry!" whispered Ros nervously.

In another three minutes Ray had Ros free, then the latter released Bart. All three lads gave a surprised start when they heard the muffled purr of a powerful motor. Headlight beams cut a bright swathe through the cabin window, lighting up the wall, then disappearing as a car swung around outside.

"Keep your hands behind your back," warned Ray.

In a moment heavy steps sounded on the gravel and three men shouldered into the room.

"We've got Lacey!" exclaimed Horton. "What do we do with him?"

Straber, the lean, swarthy man Ray and Ros had noticed in the *Triton's* lounge on the evening of the robbery, stepped forward. For a moment a savage gleam of satisfaction made his black eyes brilliant, then he uttered a roar of anger.

"That isn't Lacey, you fools! It's those kids from that ball team from the states!"

"But Straber—" protested Horton.

"Here goes!" shouted Ray, his glance flicking warningly to his chums.

His right hand swooped to his coat pocket, gripped the seams of a baseball he carried there. With a concerted cry the three boys lurched to their feet. Ray's arm was cocked, then it shot forward and the white sphere hummed across the cabin.

Straber was stumbling backward, clawing at the gun he carried in a shoulder holster when the baseball struck him right between the eyes and knocked him down like a fallen tree. Brigham snarled and flung up his gun. Red flame gushed from the black muzzle and a scream-ing bullet whined over Ray's head. Then the coura-geous lad charged full into the man, his head ramming into Brigham's chin and snapping his teeth together. At the same time Ros and Bart grappled with Horton in a savage encounter that spilled chairs all about the room.

Brigham's knees buckled and he swayed drunkenly. He lashed out wildly with a right fist and caught Ray behind the ear, dazing him momentarily. A straight jab landed against Ray's teeth, then he caught the fleeting vision of dark shoe leather, aimed in a wicked kick at his stomach.

Somehow Ray lurched to one side, caught that arcing foot in firm hands and jerked Brigham off his feet. The renegade spilled to the floor in an ungainly heap, his head striking the edge of a chair as he collapsed, rendering him unconscious.

Ray quickly joined his two chums but found his as-sistance was not needed. Ros and Bart had clubbed Horton into submission.

"Good work, boys!" said Ray, wiping a shirt sleeve across his perspiring face.

"Good work!" repeated Ros, admiringly. "Look what you did! You took care of two of them while we were subduing this snake."

"What now?" demanded Bart, grinning his enjoyment of the short physical encounter with Straber and his two henchmen.

"Straber came in a car. If it was a sedan, we'll truss these fellows up, pile them in the back and try to find our way back to Havana and a police station."

"Let's go," urged Ros, "before these skunks come out of their artificial sleep. Besides, Ames and the rest are probably worried sick, wondering what became of us."

Without wasting further time in idle conversation the three boys, using the same ropes with which they themselves had been bound, quickly trussed up Straber, Horton and Brigham. Then, working in relays, they transported the limp forms of the renegades to the back of Straber's car which proved to be a sedan. Ros and Bart stayed in the rear, keeping close watch over their captives while Ray got behind the wheel.

In a short time they had rolled clear of the rutted side road and were humming along a paved highway, headed back in the direction they thought led to Havana. And they proved to be right. As they left the country behind and approached more populous quarters, they inquired of several people how to reach a police station.

They were about to abandon hope of securing the information, when they met a policeman who could talk and understand English. He was amazed at the news of what they had done and quickly hopped in the car.

Ten minutes later the car was parked in front of a small police precinct building, and Straber and his cronies were being led inside. Ray told his story to the tall, brown-skinned official in charge of the station. As he concluded the tale, there was a great stir of activity among other policemen. Orders were given. Telephone calls were made and men ran back and forth.

"You boys did fine work tonight," complimented the head official. "We shall hold these men for further investigation. We are wiring the authorities back in New York City to check on these men to see if they are wanted on any charges."

In the course of the story it was impossible for Ray to keep from bringing John Lacey's name into the discussion. However, Ray did his utmost to impress upon the Cuban police that Lacey had been more of a dupe for the gang than anything else, and that he was intent on casting all such activities out of his life.

The police appeared to understand the situation, but explained that it would be necessary to hold Lacey for questioning. Therefore, a policeman was dispatched to the *Triton* for the steward, while several others departed in an official car for the gang's hideout to search the premises for stolen loot.

Sometime later Ray managed to get to a telephone and make a connection with the hotel at which the All-Stars were staying. He left instructions for Jimmy Ames to be paged and finally the Clarkville coach came on the wire.

Ames was immensely relieved when he heard the boys were safe. Then, as the tale unfolded over the telephone, he gasped in amazement at the adventures the three lads had experienced.

"That settles it," stormed Ames, when Ray had finished. "There'll be no more tours until we're safely back in the U. S. A. From now on I'm not going to leave you fellows out of my sight. We're all back at the hotel and I want you boys to return at once. You're all going to bed and stay there, if I have to sleep outside your door all night to see that you don't get in any more scrapes. Why you might have been killed—"

Ames's voice droned on and on but Ray wasn't listening. He had hung up and now he turned to Ros and Bart.

"Ames is all steamed up. He wants us to come right to the hotel."

"Well, I'm ready," said Ros.

"Wait!" said Bart. His cheeks were flushed and his lip trembled a trifle. He extended his hand. "I'm afraid I've been ten kinds of a fool. I've hated you, Ray and you, Ros and that chap, Bert West. I'm sorry for that. What happened tonight sort of opened my eyes. I'm grateful for what you chaps did."

"Forget it," said Ray, smiling warmly.

"Friends?" queried Bart tensely.

"You bet!" answered Ray and Ros together as the boys solemnly shook hands, cementing a new and greater friendship between them.

CHAPTER XIX

THE ALL-STAR GAME

JIM CRESSET, second baseman from Springfield, and lead-off man for the American nine, swung at the first pitch and punched it deep into right field where the Cuban fielder camped under it for the out, and the All-Star contest was underway.

Alex Raquel was hurling for the Cuban All-Stars while Bart Himber was to handle the pitching chores for the American squad for four or five innings. The stadium was packed with white-shirted baseball fans, all of them cheering for the home team, and keeping up a tremendous din of sound so that the infield chatter and the idle banter from the bench could not be heard. Now that the game had started, Ames and Mallory sat tensely beside one another, their eyes drinking in every movement on the spotless diamond.

For three solid innings Raquel stopped the American All-Stars cold. Not even Ray could get a hit, though he drove a long ball into center field which was caught ten feet from the fence. Bart Himber matched the Cuban in the first two frames, hurling even more superbly than his rival, and retiring five of the batters to face him on strikes.

But Bart was trying too hard and he ran into trouble when he faced the lower third of the Cuban line-up. The shortstop cracked out a hit into center field. The catcher followed with a vicious grounder which Jim Cresset knocked down, then tossed over Al Torrance's head in his haste to get a force on the runner from first.

With all hands safe Raquel pumped a double into the hole between right and center. The Cuban hurler scored a few moments later on an infield out and a long fly. Bart then retired the side by fanning the next batter.

Ray and the others hustled in from the diamond at the start of the fourth faced with the necessity of overcoming a three-run deficit.

"Here we go, fellows!" cried Ray. "Let's get some runs."

"Don't mind those runs," said Ros to Bart, who appeared downcast. "We're going to win this ball game."

"That's the spirit," broke in Fred Dressen. Ray and Ros looked at the latter, surprised and secretly pleased at the change in the Springfield backstop. Dressen gulped nervously then went on: "Bart told me about last night and I want you to know I'd like to be friends, too, though not just on account of what you fellows did. I've been a heel, but I'd like to make amends."

"I'm your friend," responded Ray quickly. "You can count on that."

"Thanks," said Dressen. "From now on we'll work together."

"And by working together as a unit is just how we're going to beat this Cuban outfit," was Ros' firm opinion.

Mallory, after a discussion with Ames, instructed Jim Cresset to lay down a bunt. The latter did so, but the bunt was not well placed and Raquel threw him out. Then Al Torrance struck out and there were two away. The hopes of the American All-Stars began to look slim indeed.

Ros missed two wide, sweeping curves, then took a tight grip on his bat and shot a hot grounder to the left of the third baseman. The latter stopped the ball but was unable to make the throw and it was scored as a hit. A wild roar lifted from the Americans' bench, then, as Ray trudged to the plate. It was a fierce battle cry that struggled for recognition against the strident yelling of the partisan crowd.

Once again Raquel, working with amazing deftness and cunning, slipped two fast strikes over on Ray to put him in a hole. But the Cuban made a mistake in trying to slip another one past Ray. The Clarkville left fielder put all the fierce power of his shoulder and wrist muscles into his swing. He forgot the pain in his wrists which were raw from working free of his bonds. He forgot everything but the wild elation that came with the knowledge that he had met the ball squarely and that it was soaring far over the outfield.

There was never any doubt where that ball was going. Even the Cuban fans roared their pleasure as the gleaming white sphere disappeared beyond the right field barrier, and Ray sprinted around the bases behind Ros. Ray was greeted by wild cheers and firm handclasps from his teammates when he crossed the plate.

"That puts us definitely back in the game," said Dressen and proceeded to wallop a three-bagger over the centerfielder's head.

But no other run scored because Raquel took a hitch in his belt, turned on the steam and whiffed Frank Duane, the first baseman from Glendale for the final out.

The Cubans came back in their half of the fourth and tallied once more. The first batter dragged out a perfect bunt and made first safely. After stealing second and languishing there while Bart retired the next two men, the runner scored on a fluke double that dropped between Jim Cresset and Ros in short center field. Bart prevented further trouble by inducing the next batter to pop to Fred Dressen three feet in front of the plate.

Clarkville was helpless at the plate in the fifth. Bill Scully followed Ed Hinkle's infield out with a line single over second, but never got any farther, for Tom Raynor, who came in to bat for Bart, and Jim Cresset, both sent long fly balls to the outfield. Thus the score remained 4 to 2 in favor of the Cuban All-Stars.

The Cubans, however, scored once more in their half of the same inning. Tom, who was now hurling in place of Bart, had difficulty locating the plate, and walked the first two batters to face him. Ray made a sensational catch of a line drive close to the left field foul line. Then the Cubans worked a daring double steal as Tom threw a floater to the next batter.

Fred Dressen leaped up and pegged the ball down to Bill Scully and the runner slid into the bag amid a huge cloud of dust. It was a very close play and the umpire ruled the runner safe. Both Ames and Mallory rushed out to protest the decision, and the Americans' infield joined the crush around third base.

However, all arguments were wasted, and Ames and Mallory were forced to return to the bench while the play remained as originally called. The picture looked a trifle brighter when Bill Scully grabbed a hot grounder and rifled it to Fred Dressen to cut down a potential run at the plate. That made it two out, but Tom couldn't get past Alex Raquel, who besides being a fine pitcher, was also talented as a slugger. With a count of three-and-two on him, Raquel pasted a fast one over second for a clean single to raise the score to 5 to 2. Then Tom braced, inducing the Cubans' lead-off batter to loft an infield fly to Frank Duane at first.

Once again the American All-Stars, still undaunted

by this turn of fortune, came racing in briskly from the diamond, eyes bright with determination and hope. They were all youngsters, but the spirit of combat, the will to win, burned fiercely in their veins.

And once again it was Ray, playing the greatest game of his career, who lifted the hopes of his teammates—this time with another tremendous round-tripper with the base paths empty. No one else could hit safely in that frame, but at least the American boys had crept one run closer to a tie score.

Tom held the Cubans scoreless in the sixth and, after the boys from the U. S. A. failed to dent the plate with runs in the seventh, Tom again breezed through a perfect inning. With Fred Dressen calling the signals carefully, drawing the best out of Tom with every pitch, the Clarkville boy showed his mettle, improving as the game wore on. His fast ball had a bewildering hop, his curve was breaking sharply, and he was fooling the Cubans with a tantalizing change of pace.

The eighth inning was also scoreless on both sides as Raquel and Tom matched each other pitch for pitch. Coming in for the top half of the ninth and on the short end of 5 to 3 count, the Americans dug in and prepared to make a last-ditch fight of it.

Ros proved to be Raquel's first victim, fouling out to the third baseman. After him came Ray with the din of those packed stands pounding his ears. Glancing toward the bench, he saw his teammates waving to him, urging him to hit another home run. He set himself firmly at the plate, watching Raquel set himself, teeter back on his heels, then whip his body forward in a smooth, swift motion.

The ball was a blurred mass of white, twirling end over end and plunking into the catcher's mitt as Ray brought his bat around and missed for strike one. Raquel wasted two, trying to nick the outside corner, then pulled the string on one. Ray topped the pitch and sent it trickling outside the third base line and the count was evened at 2-and-2.

The Cubans in the stand were chanting now, but the boys sitting near Ames and Mallory were taut and still. What Ray did at this moment might easily decide the outcome of this game.

And then it happened. There was the resounding thump of willow connecting with horsehide. The outfielders were running and Ray was streaking down the first base line. He rounded first, then slowed to a trot when he saw how the centerfielder threw down his glove in disgust while the ball plummeted over the fence. And with the cheers of the All-Americans still contesting the shouts of the Cubans for Raquel to turn on the steam, Fred Dressen stepped up and blasted another four-master to tie the score at 5-all.

"What a wallop, Fred!" erupted Ray, gripping the catcher's hand. "I knew you'd do it."

"What about yourself, Ray," countered Fred with a

grin. "You've hit three home runs in this game. You're going like a house afire!"

"They'll never stop us now," breathed Bart, his face flushed with pleasure.

"I guess we've got Raquel's number now," chanted the rest of the squad, waiting for Frank Duane to hit.

CHAPTER XX

HOME RUN HENNESSEY

RAY was about to join the happy chorus of assent when he felt a light pressure on his arm and he whirled around.

"Lacey! This is a surprise," he said.

The steward grinned and shook hands fervently with Ray, Ros, Bart and Tom.

"How is everything?" queried Ros.

"Fine. Thanks to you chaps," murmured Lacey. "I've heard all about your experience with Straber and his two pals and you fellows sure turned the city upside down. You're heroes!"

"We were lucky," said Bart.

"Perhaps," grunted Lacey. "But luck or not I'm in your debt for taking three snakes off my trail. I've been with the police all morning until about an hour ago, answering all kinds of questions."

"Any news?" Ray wanted to know.

"Plenty. The police recovered all the loot at Straber's hideout. It appears that all the stuff—and most of it was jewelry—was too *hot* to handle right away and they were waiting for the excitement of some of their

robberies to wear off before trying to dispose of the booty.

"The New York police have wired Havana to hold all three men pending arrival of special detectives to bring them back to the states to face charges of theft, burglary and extortion. It seems they were implicated in more than one shady deal."

"But what about yourself?" inquired Ray tensely.

Lacey's face sobered. "I have to stay here for further questioning, but I don't think the police will hold me. Captain Blaine has promised to speak for me."

"And your job?"

"That's safe, too. And I'm glad. From now on I'm going to be content to earn my money the hard way."

"Well, in your case there were unusual circumstances," said Ros. "After all, your mother was seriously ill."

"That's true," replied Lacey soberly. "But it never pays to step outside the law. I guess if it hadn't been for you fellows I might not even be here to thank you. No telling what Straber might have done."

"Well, it's all over," said Ray, grinning. "You can start from scratch. As for Straber, I guess he'll do all his scheming in jail from now on."

Ames' strident voice broke into their animated conversation.

"Out on the diamond, you fellows. The Cubans are batting."

Ray whirled in confusion. He had been so intent

upon Lacey's recital, that for the moment he had forgotten about the ball game. The fact that the Cubans were coming to bat in the last of the ninth, and that there had been no further cheering from the Americans' bench, told him that Duane and Hinkle had been retired by Raquel.

Tie score! The last half of the ninth inning. Would the game go on into the tenth? Or, would Tom Raynor crack and yield the lonely tally necessary to give the Cubans victory? That was the question disturbing every player. But Tom did not crack. Putting his heart and soul into every toss, he mowed down the side in the ninth. And in the tenth Bill Scully, Tom Raynor and Jim Cresset went down swinging as Raquel put everything he had into his pitching.

In the last half of the tenth Tom lost a bit of his magic, walking one Cuban with two out. The next batter rifled a hard-hit ball over the shortstop's head. Ray charged in like an express locomotive to make a dazzling pick-up. Without halting his forward drive, he whipped the ball underhand to Bill Scully at third, and the runner who had started for that base, scurried back to second. The danger passed, however, when the next batter slashed a hot liner, chest-high, right into the gloved hand of Jim Cresset at the keystone sack.

The game dragged on into the eleventh. Ames and Mallory were tense and haggard.

"Any special instructions, coach?" queried Al Torrance, the shortstop from Bridgeport, as he prepared to lead off for the American All-Stars.

"Get on base. That's all," snapped Ames impatiently.

Torrance nodded and strode away. The boy was nervous and he showed it by biting at a wide curve and missing it. Raquel was calm and poised. He shot over a high one which Torrance let go by, then came in with a swift cross-fire pitch which Torrance smacked on the handle of his bat. The result was a weak pop-up to Raquel a few feet in front of the mound.

Ros then prepared to take his turn at the plate. He hit a long foul into the stands behind the third base line, let two wide ones go by, then backed the left fielder up to the fence with a prodigious drive. Unfortunately the outfielder nabbed the ball and there were two gone.

"Park one, Ray!" pleaded his teammates as Ray followed Ros to the plate.

"Go ahead, Ray. Blast it! Do what I couldn't do," murmured Ros dejectedly.

Ray looked at Ames, saw the pleading, hopeful look in the man's eyes, and suddenly felt the perspiration seep out of his pores. They were all looking for him to win the game. There were two out and everyone had noticed that Tom was weakening out there on the hill. He might just possibly get by the eleventh, but not the twelfth. In the meantime, the American All-Stars needed a run.

That knowledge and the fact that it all rested on his shoulders made Ray tremble. He glanced out at the poised but grim figure of Alex Raquel on the mound. The latter would put his whole heart into every pitch. He wouldn't give Ray anything good to hit at.

Ray shook himself out of his somber reverie as he caught the fleeting vision of Raquel's arm in motion. But Ray was over-anxious, and swung too soon on an inside pitch missing it by inches. The next one looked good, but it dropped deceptively as it shot across the plate and Ray topped it for a foul.

Again there was the wind-up, the long sweep of arm, the humming white sphere racing toward him. Crack! Ray met the ball with savage power, then groaned as the tremendous fly cleared the right field fence, three feet on the wrong side of the foul line. And still he was in a hole against Raquel.

Then the Cuban missed the inside corner for a ball. The next was chest-high but a little wide, and Ray held his breath tensely while the umpire signalled it was a ball. Two-and-two was the count. What would the next pitch be?

There it came, hurtling toward the plate! It looked like a straight fast ball. The bat moved off Ray's shoulders in a smooth arc. At the last moment Ray saw the humming sphere break sharply away from himself. But the pitch did not break swiftly enough, and Ray connected on the very end of his bat, feeling a hot tingle in his arms when the ball gyrated toward the sky as if shot from a cannon.

Far and deep it went between left and center field. Both fielders sprinted toward the fence. Right up against the barrier they flung themselves, gloved hands outstretched, then falling back limply as the white horsehide eluded their fingertips and dropped over the fence for Ray's fourth home run of the day!

After that tremendous blow it didn't matter that Fred Dressen flied out to end the inning, or that the Cubans still had a turn at bat in the last half of the eleventh. The American All-Stars were jubilant. The infielders chattered constantly. The outfielders called back and forth to one another.

"It's 6 to 5, boys!" yelled Ros, "and that's the way the score is going to remain."

"Come on, Tom," cried Bill Scully to the pitcher. "Just three up and three down."

Tom grinned and faced the first batter. He hurled a ball, a strike, then another ball and another strike and still another ball. There was the smashing sound of wood meeting horsehide and the ball went zooming out over Tom's head. The next moment there was an amazed cry from the stands as Al Torrance leaped high into the air to make a one-handed stab of the ball.

What this catch meant to the Americans was appreciated a few seconds later when Alex Raquel punched a double into deep left field. If Torrance had failed to make the catch of that high liner, the score would have been tied by Raquel's safety.

Everyone grew tense as Tom, perspiration streaming down his face in the great heat, toiled to retire the next batter. Again it went to a full count. Tom was tiring now and his arm felt like lead. But he gritted his teeth, pouring in the next pitch which was smashed down to Jim Cresset at second. Cresset took the ball on one hop and rifled it to first for the out, Raquel scampering to third.

Ray played his position deeper as Trachado, a hard hitting outfielder from the city of Santiago, Cuba, came up to the plate. He was a big, rangy fellow and he struck at the first pitch, walloping it high and far into left field. Ray whirled at the crack of the bat, put his back to the plate and raced toward the fence. Dirt flew in clods from his churning spikes as that grim race between ball and player went on.

There was a dull, sinking sensation in the pit of Ray's stomach as he realized that if he failed to make this catch, the ball game would be lost. Even at the crack of the bat, the hit had had all the earmarks of being a home run.

But still Ray bolted across the turf. Suddenly the slatted boards of the fence loomed directly in front of him. He thrust his head up, saw the ball dropping down swiftly. He leaped high into the air, climbing halfway up the fence, body twisting in a half turn, gloved hand stretched toward the whirling horsehide.

He felt a solid shock in his glove, then he see-sawed precariously on the rim of the flat barrier, finally sliding down the inside slats to the ground, the ball still gripped firmly in his mitt.

Dimly he realized the game was over and that the American All-Stars had won the contest 6 to 5 in a breath-taking thriller. Suddenly he was mobbed by his own teammates. They were shouting and yelling incoherently. He was being dragged across the diamond. He caught the blur of familiar, grinning faces—Ros, Tom, Bart, Fred, the two coaches. Everyone was talking at once.

"What a ball game!"

"Will we have something to talk about when we get home!"

"Three cheers for Ray—the home run ace!"

"Hurrah! Four home runs in one day!"

Ros and Tom and the two new friends, Bart and Fred, finally got Ray to themselves, though others of the team were looking on as they moved through the press of the crowd toward their dressing quarters.

"From now on," said Bart with a pleased grin, "we're calling you Home Run Hennessey!"

"And don't say the title doesn't fit," added Fred Dressen in mock warning. "Any fellow that can hit four home runs in succession against a pitcher of Raquel's ability must be good."

"Thanks, fellows," said Ray with a laugh. "But don't forget we all helped to win this game. It was team work that won after all."

"Now that we've conquered Havana," said Ros, "let's invade the good old U. S. A."

"You bet. America, here we come!" shouted a host of happy voices.

Gradually the American All-Stars, pushing and shoving their way through the crowd that had flooded the diamond immediately after the final out, gained the quiet of their own quarters. But into the din of the crowd's excited yelling and talking, drifted one triumphant shout and it came from the boys who had invaded the tropics.

"Three cheers for Home Run Hennessey!"

THE END